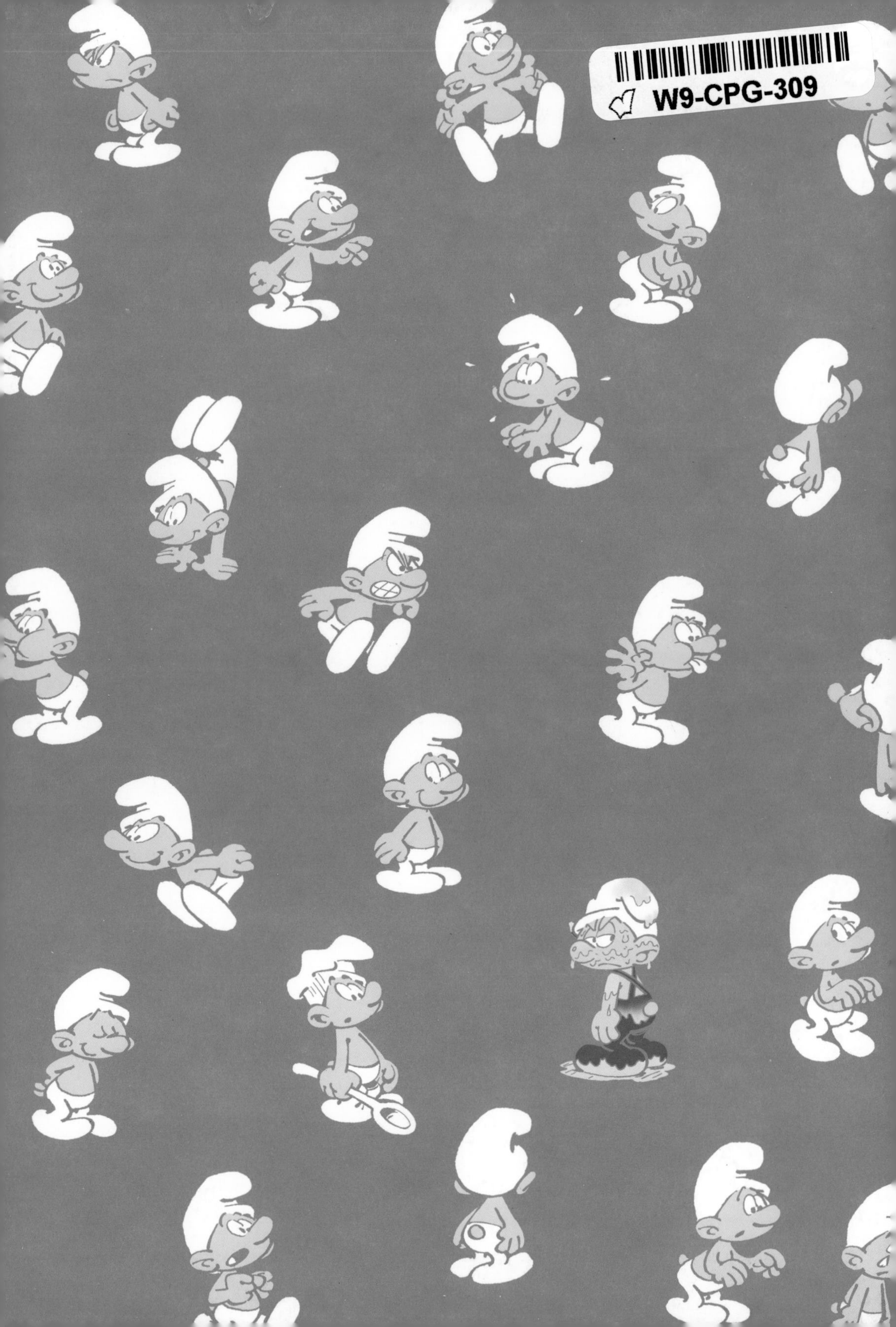

THE SMURFS TALES

Peyo

PAPERCUT Z
MIAMI

THE SMURFS TALES #7

The Smurfs were born in 1958 in Belgium. Benny Breakiron was created in 1960. These stories respect the artwork and writing as originally created per the wishes of the authors and their publisher. However, they may contain outdated cultural depictions and gun violence. Rather than remove this content, we want to acknowledge its harmful impact, learn from it, and spark conversation to create a more inclusive future together.

© *Peyo* - 2023 - Licensed through Lafig Belgium - www.smurf.com

SMURF™

English translation copyright © 2023 by Mad Cave Studios and Papercutz.
All rights reserved.

"The Giant Smurfs"
BY PEYO
WITH THE COLLABORATION OF
ALAIN JOST, THIERRY CULLIFORD AND POET SMURF FOR THE SCRIPT,
PASCAL GARRAY FOR THE ARTWORK,
AND NINE CULLIFORD FOR THE COLORS

"The Magic Doll"
BY PEYO AND ALBERT BLESTEAU

"Smurferries 2"
BY PEYO

Joe Johnson and Nanette McGuinness, *SMURFLATIONS*
Bryan Senka and Justin Birch, *LETTERING SMURFS*
Léa Zimmerman, *SMURFIC PRODUCTION*
Matt. Murray, *SMURF CONSULTANT*
Stephanie Brooks, *ASSISTANT SMURF*
Zohra Ashpari, *EDITOR SMURF*
Rex Ogle, *SMURFITORIAL DIRECTOR*
Jim Salicrup, *SMURF-IN-CHIEF*

PAPERCUTZ WAS FOUNDED BY TERRY NANTIER AND JIM SALICRUP.

HC ISBN 978-1-5458-1030-9
PB ISBN 978-1-5458-1031-6

PRINTED IN CHINA
MAY 2023

FIRST PAPERCUTZ PRINTING

THE GIANT SMURFS

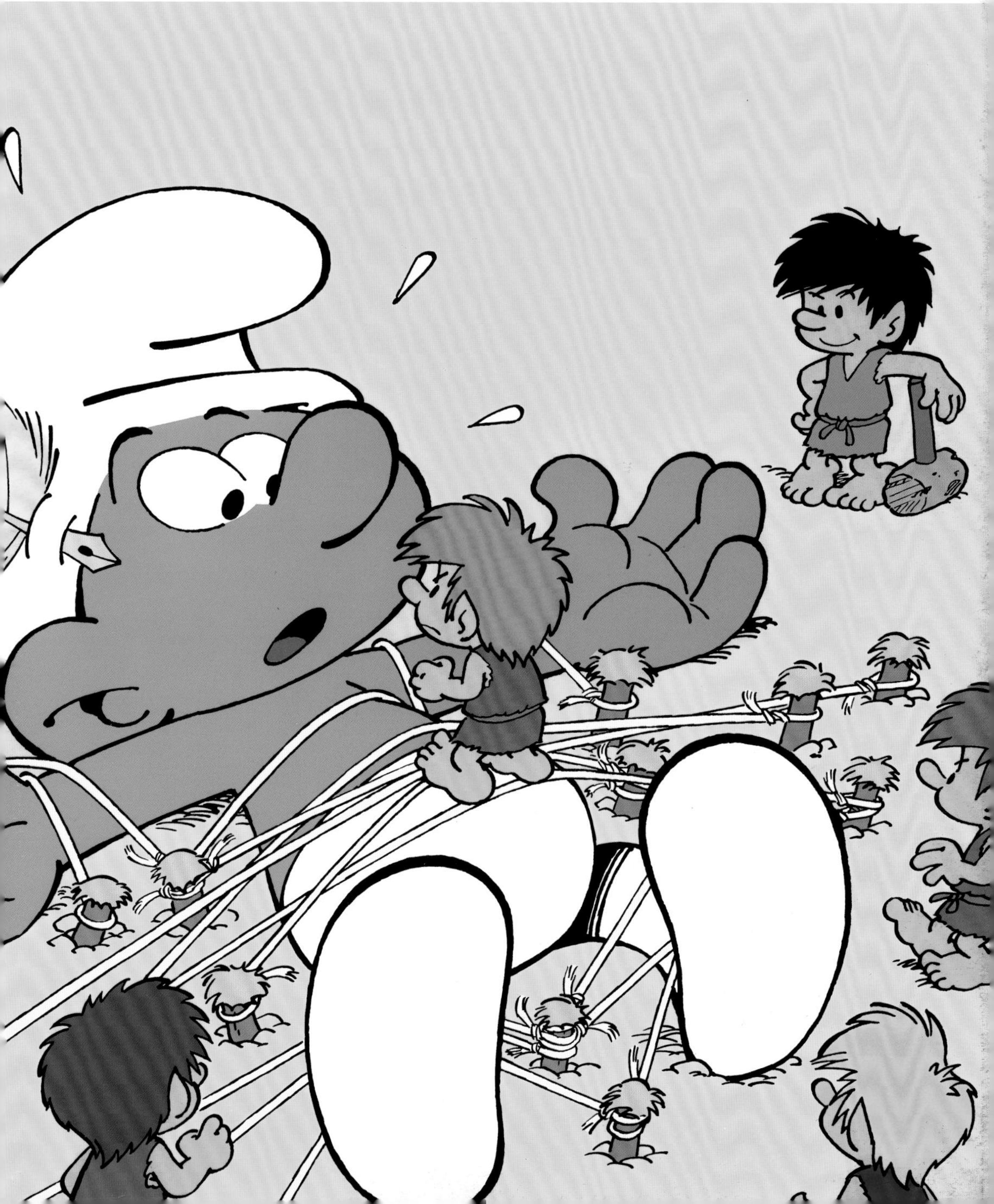

A peaceful summer afternoon in the land of the smurfs...

AHAHAAA!
!

THIS TIME YOU WON'T ESCAPE ME!

Quick! Let's smurf in there!

Oh! Excuse us!

?

I saw you! ♪ ♫

And there's no way out. I've got you now!

Oh, how I relish this moment!

OOUUCH!

You filthy beast! That huuurt!

Run! Time to smurf your personal record!

I think we lost him!

Yes, we smurfed away right under his nose once again!

Even so, I'm smurfed up with running away from that stupid wizard! If we weren't so small, I'd smurf my fist in his smurf!

You're right, Hefty Smurf! It would really be smurf if we could be giants, too!

Yes, but we'd show respect for folks littler than us! We Smurfs aren't brutes like Gargamel!

Well, let's smurf to the village! We're small and that won't change.

No, but I like the idea!

Aren't you coming to eat, Poet Smurf?

Later. I have two or three things to smurf onto paper!

Yes...I feel like I'm going to smurf an epic work!

RICH RHYMES

SCRITCH SCRITCH

Poet Smurf didn't come... Is he sick?

No, I think he's busy writing another of his smurfing poems!

I smurfed the start of a true Smurf saga! Do you want to hear it?

Uh...

>Meh!<

Let me smurf the amazing adventure
That six daring young Smurfs once did venture.
On a rickety skiff, they sailed off one day
'Long the wide River Smurf, they went gliding away.

They were carefree, joyful, and quite delirious...
Yet the pathways of fate are mysterious!
The river, so calm now, suddenly surged:
From the furious waves quite far did they next emerge.

Well! I'm going to bed! I have to smurf up early tomorrow!

I still have a little project to smurf!

Look... I love great stories, but after a long day, I don't want to smurf my brain! Smurf us some fantasy, action, exciting battles... None of this *blahblahblah!*

Yeah, Poet Smurf, what he said! If you want a smurfing audience, you have to respond to popular demand...

Okay, I get it! I'll smurf down to their level!

The following days, Poet Smurf rarely went out...

Will you come smurf a walk with us?

No, I'm working!

I have to smurf back to work!

?

He worked intensely...

He wasn't very sociable...

Paper! Smurf me some paper!

Finally, one morning...

Brainy Smurf, do you want to read my story?

Of course! Smurf it to me!

Here! Handy Smurf smurfed it for me!

For smurfs' sake! It's a real brick!

Give me your honest opinion of it!

You can trust me to do that!

Smurf! If I have to read all this, it'll smurf me the whole day!

ZEEE ZEEE ZEEE

WAAAAAH!

Hmm! Here won't work! They're smurfing too much noise!

TOC TOC TOC

PWEEEET

I'm going smurf to the forest where it's nice and calm.

There! I'll be fine here!

"The Giant Smurfs"... A story about Smurfs?! Crazy idea!

Huh? For once, he didn't smurf in verse...

One fine morning, a group of Smurfs went off to smurf a journey along the river. Handy Smurf had smurfed a new boat design...

You're sure it won't be dangerous? I can't swim very well!

You've got nothing to smurf about!

With these barrels smurfed on the sides, my new boat will be unsinkable!

Un-- what?

It can't smurf, you ignoramus!

Igno-- what?

Come aboard, yellow-belly! There aren't any storms on our fine River Smurf!

Cast off the lines, mateys! I'll smurf the sail!

8

Meanwhile, back at the dam...

There! The leak is smurfed! I'll go back up!

The leak was very tiny.

Yes, but tiny leaks smurf big floods!

That's why we should smurf repairs immediately!

You see, a dam is a smurfly dangerous structure and--

For smurfs' sake! These ropes **ALWAYS** have to get caught!

Ah, there... It's free!

As I was saying, this dam can be very dangerous if we smurf at all carelessly!

On the river...

Has anyone seen my trumpet?

A trumpet?

Th-There's a huge wave smurfing toward us!

It's just a hallucination! The sun has smurfed his brain!

SO IS THIS A HALLUCINATION?!

Disaster! The dam must have smurfed!

Hang on!

The sail! We have to smurf the sail!

CRAC

BING

There, it's smurfed for good!

Hey! I found my trumpet!

Great! Then everything's okay!

Smurf course! We have to get to the shore!

Impossible! I can't steer anymore!

6

But that dam is also very useful. Since we smurfed it, we've been able to control the river flow!

Speaking of river flow... The current is smurfly strong, don't you think?

?

THE SLUICE GATE!
It's open!

Quick -- we have to resmurf it right away!

Who's the clueless Smurf who did that?!

⇥Phew!⇤ I hope it didn't smurf too much damage...

Hey! It looks like it's calming down...

Yes, the current is less smurfy!

I wonder what happened at the dam...

Anyway, we smurfed a speed record!

We're really far from the village!

Yes! And the countryside is smurfy pretty!

It'sh true! Why don't we ushually come here?

Yes, well, it's because of the waterfall!

THE WATERFALL!

TOO LATE! We're smurfing right into it!

AAAAAH!

SPLASH

Incredible! We're past the waterfall!

And we're safe and smurf!

I told you! My boat is unsinkable!

Unsink-- what?

Fluctuat nec smurfitur! It sways but doesn't sink!

Wait... Three... Four... There're five of us! Someone's missing!

8

⇒Gulp!⇐
Help!

The shore...
I have to smurf to
the shore...

No, I can't
reach it! I'm on
my last legs!
⇒Glug!⇐

Oh, cruel destiny!
Was it my fate that in this
furious flood, I'd smurf
my last sigh?

No! That would be
too great a loss for
Smurf poetry!

Saved! But
I really thought
my last hour had
smurfed!

I've got that one over
there!

We need to go
back up the river and
find Poet Smurf!

I hope he
didn't drown!
He swims like a
lead smurf!

13

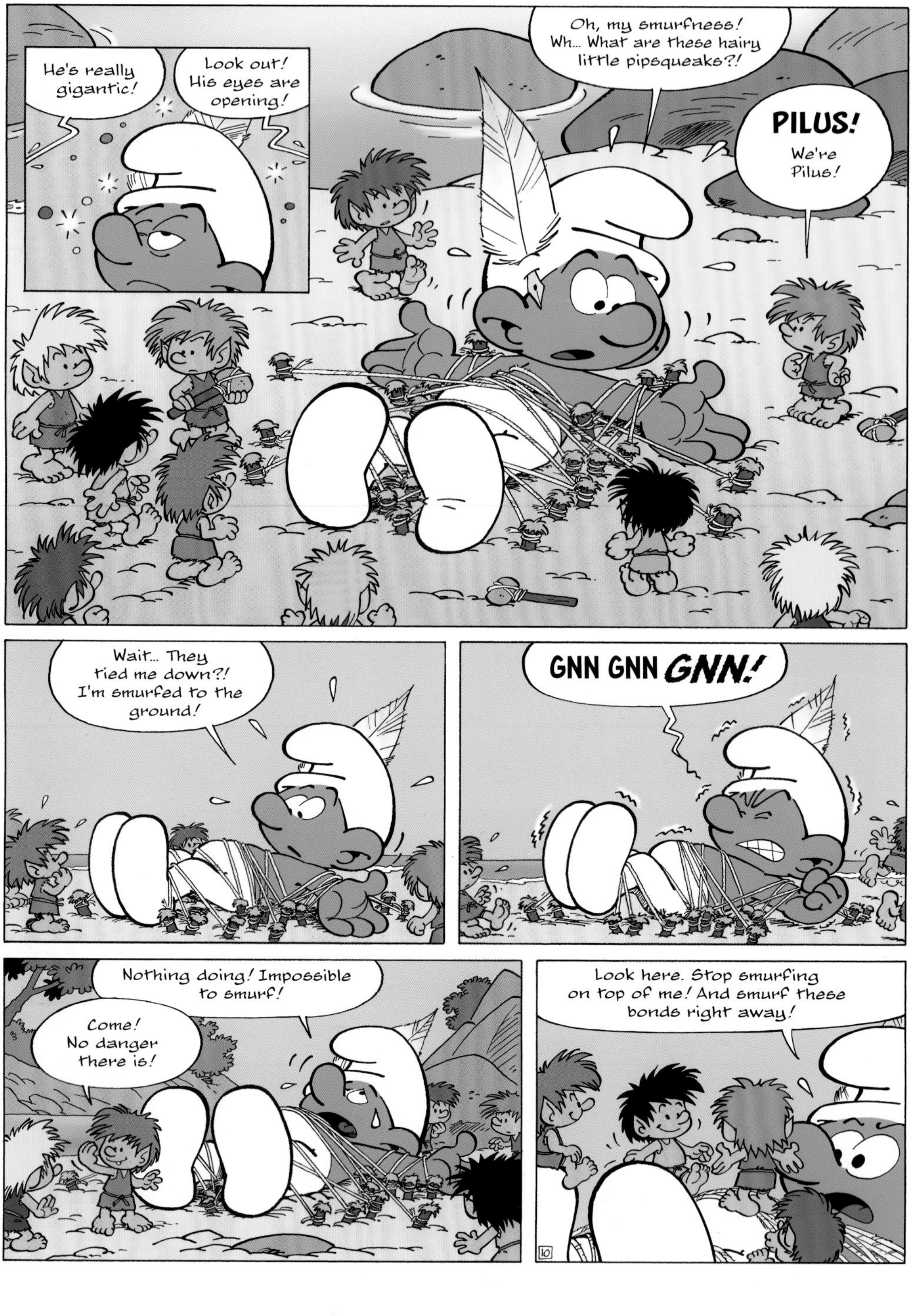
He's really gigantic!
Look out! His eyes are opening!
Oh, my smurfness! Wh... What are these hairy little pipsqueaks?!
PILUS! We're Pilus!
Wait... They tied me down?! I'm smurfed to the ground!
GNN GNN GNN!
Nothing doing! Impossible to smurf!
Come! No danger there is!
Look here. Stop smurfing on top of me! And smurf these bonds right away!
10

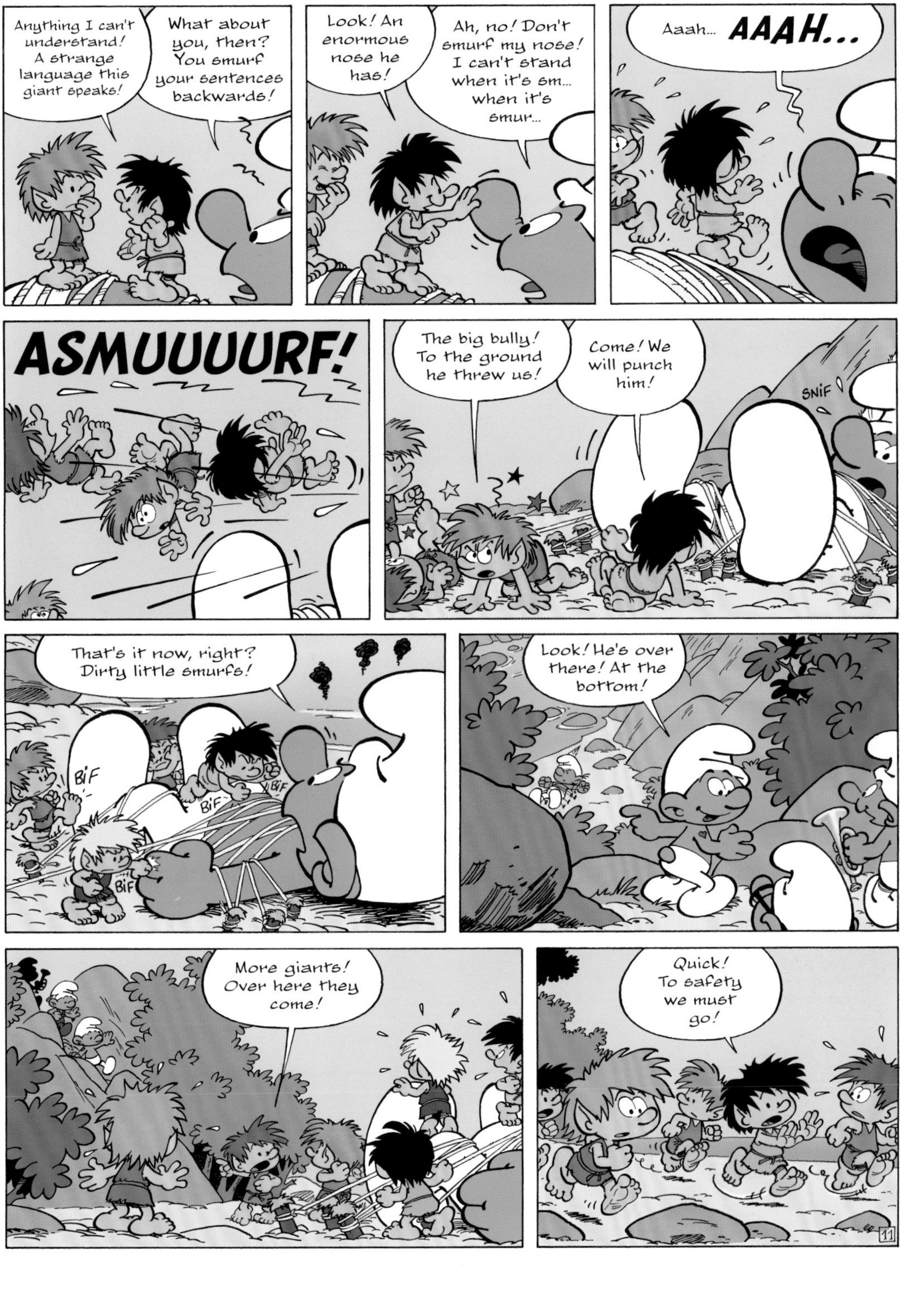
Anything I can't understand! A strange language this giant speaks!
What about you, then? You smurf your sentences backwards!
Look! An enormous nose he has!
Ah, no! Don't smurf my nose! I can't stand when it's sm... when it's smur...
Aaah... AAAH...
ASMUUUURF!
The big bully! To the ground he threw us!
Come! We will punch him!
SNIF
That's it now, right? Dirty little smurfs!
BIF
BIF
BIF
BIF
Look! He's over there! At the bottom!
More giants! Over here they come!
Quick! To safety we must go!
11

Are you okay Poet Smurf? Nothing smurfed?

No, but get me free, quickly!

Who did this? You've been smurfed up like a sausage!

Mini men! They say they're Pilus! I'd fainted and they took the opportunity to smurf me up with ropes!

≾Phew!≿ That feels good! My legs were beginning to smurf!

They're tiny? Even compared to us?!

Amazing! I'd like to get a closer smurf at them!

I saw them run away! They all smurfed that way!

Nothing... But they couldn't have smurfed very far!

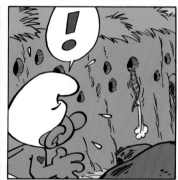

!

Ahaaa! Someone's smurfing in there!

Oh, it's smurfable! They're nesting in these little caves!

Come on, little Pilu! Smurf out of your hole! We want to see you!

No way! Big folks I don't trust!

You're going to smurf out of there, by hook or by crook!

ARGH!

OW! That little piece of smurf bit me!

I'm going to smurf you a lesson!

NO! Stop!

Even though they're very little, we shouldn't take advantage of our strength! It would disgrace Smurfs! As Papa Smurf always says, "Don't smurf to others what you wouldn't want them to smurf to you!"

Pilus, we come in peace! We won't smurf you any harm! We just want to smurf friendly ties between our two people!

Yes... Pretty speech at the start they make...

And afterwards little people they squash!

To speak with you I will!

Worthy of trust you are! In your eyes I see it!

That's right, it's all in the eyes!

PiluPen my name is! Scribe of the Pilus I am!

I'm Brainy Smurf, the Smurf scholar! Pleased to meet you!

Come on, let's sit down! We can smurf... uh, talk more comfortably!

Why did you tie me up? That wasn't very smurf of you!

Near our camp a giant we found... Dangerous for us you could be!

13

At our summer camp we are! From our city in the mountains we came down seeds to collect! Because only seeds we eat!

What do they collect? He's smurfing randomly!

He says they only smurf seeds!

No wonder they're so teenie-weenie!

We Smurfs smurf in a village in the middle of the forest! We smurfed here accidentally!

Zmurf... Zmurfed... Anything I don't understand!

A primitive language that must be!

In the caves the Pilus live! In Pilulit, our city, into the rock they are dug!

We smurf our homes in the shape of mushrooms!

Mushrooms?! Why?

Strange ideas you have!

Of course not! We love mushrooms! They're smurfingly good to eat!

WHAT? Mushrooms you eat?!

Disgusting they are!

Not at all! Mushrooms are almost as delicious as sarsaparilla!

Sarsaparilla! Ha! Ha! Ha!

Anything these Zmurfs swallow!

Are you done now? Stop smurfing a pain!

Come on, come on! Let's smurf calm! This is just a smurf of cultures!

Right he is! Respect each other we should!

I've got an idea! We could smurf the day with you to see how you live!

Welcome you are!

These are PiluPaul, PiluPat, and PiluLuke! Seed they're going to collect!

In teams of three always we work!

Great, I'll smurf picking with you!

Come on, our treasure I'll show you!

That rock with me would you push?

Ha! Ha! Easily we moved it!

Uh... Yes! There's smurf in unity!

A nice harvest we've made! In Pilulit, very happy they'll be!

I see you write, too!

Scribe I am! Absolutely everything I write down!

I smurf poems, odes, and even plays!

Ah, no! Only dates and figures I write! In fantasy I'm not interested!

You're smurfly right, my friend! Accuracy is essential!

Every day I repeat that!

⇒Pfff!⇐ A fine pair of smurfers!

PILULI PILULA PILULILALAAA!

Is it really necessary to smurf like that?

Hooray! A nice flowery slope we've found!

Of this plant, delicious the seeds are!

Look! With this hook, the stem I grab...

Then, the dried-up flower hard I shake...

The seeds I collect!

And into the sack I pour them!

Ah, yes... It's a very smurf system!

But I can smurf the job more easily...

Whoa!

And there! By smurfing the intermediaries, it saves time!

Ouch! My sides you are squeezing!

What're these brown things?

Broom plant seed pods! Very hard to open they are!

But a great expert in this work we have!

16

Watch: the blade I slip in...

The crack I enlarge...

And... ÷GNNN...÷ HMPH... the seed pod I open!

May I?... I would smurf like this...

CRACK

And presto! The job is smurfed!

Without effort you opened it!

If I had my tools, I'd smurf a device to help you!

Never mind! We'll smurf your seed pods for you!

OH! GREEDY SMURF!

?

The task will be smurfed in a few minutes!

CRACK

Do you think these broom seed pods are good to smurf?

Upset you mustn't be! Big and strong they are, that's all!

FLAP

A good outing that was!

For us, too! Lots of mustard seeds the Smurf gathered! And the ladder we didn't need!

It's time for us to get going if we want to smurf to our village before night!

Of course not! Until tomorrow you must stay!

Yes, please stay! Soon on the seeds we'll snack!

Snack on the seeds?

Yes... Eat! Yum yum!

Ah, that's a good idea! I'm as hungry as a Smurf!

GROWL

A big pot we don't have, but lots of pig ear leaves we will grill!

Pig ear leaves? Do you think that will fill this Smurf?

Certainly not! Let's go see if there's something to smurf around here!

Where are we going to smurf the night? Their holes are too small for us!

Let's cut some branches and smurf a shelter!

The food you like?

Uh... Uh... It'sh not bad but a little dryish!

Oh?! You think so?

These Pilus smurf like birds!

CRACK CRACK

Look what we smurfed, lucky ducks: sorrel, sage...

AND SARSAPARILLA!

Great!

Delishious! Thash shomething to shmurf your teeth into! Want shome?

Thanks, no! A stomach-ache I don't want to have!

Really like rabbits they eat!

To celebrate this, I'll smurf you a little serenade!

Ah, no! Don't smurf the ears of these poor Pilus!

Of course! His music to hear we'd like!

Really? Too bad for you. You asked for it!

TARITARAAA PON TATARIRAAA SQUEAK TATAAA

BRAVO! Splendid that was!

Shivers it gave me!

What?! These Pilus are really smurf!

You know, instruments, too, we have!

Really? Go quickly and smurf them!

TARITARAAA PON SQUEAK PWAAAP PON PWAP CHICACHIC CHIC CHIC PON PON PWAAAP PON

To dance that makes me want! Not you?

Our dance you must learn! The Pilu-Pilu it's called!

Uh... We had a smurfing day! It's time for us to go to bed...

What, already?

PONNNN

It's so fun! No way to smurf an eye!

Tomorrow morning, we'll smurf here in a hurry!

Meanwhile, in the village...

They still haven't returned! This is getting smurfly worrying!

Tomorrow, we'll go look for them!

I hope nothing serious has smurfed to them!

23

Really? Already us you're leaving?

The road is long!

And Papa Smurf must be smurfing with worry!

?

!

ALEEERT! AERIAL ATTACK!

Quick! To the shelter we must go!

An attack? An attack of what?

Don't smurf questions and run!

Sparrows!

I thought an eagle was going to smurf on us!

Get away from here, you sparrows!

Go smurf seeds elsewhere!

CLAP CLAP

CLAP

The birds went away!

The giants chased them off!

20

Thanks! Our seeds you saved!

True heroes you are!

Uh... Let's not exaggerate.

It was nothing. We Smurfs are like that.

Yes, you'd better not smurf in our way!

So big and so strong you are.

With you, safe we feel.

Come on, a little longer you must stay!

Yes--To help us!

Uh... That is to say... Just a minute, then.

I think they've got us.

Well! We'll just smurf them a little helping hand and then we'll leave.

In this ditch, lots of delicious seeds we saw...

But too big the plants are...

Okay, we'll smurf them for you.

For smurfs' sake, nettles! Those sting terribly!

Wait... I think it's a dead nettle, a species that doesn't smurf!

Hey! Don't push!

Uh...

Oh! Oooh!

OOOOOH!

Ow! Ouch!

SWOOSH

Brainy Smurf! You're rotten at botany!

Ow!

Very hurt you are?

NO! I'M SMURFING UP LAUGHING!

21

Seeds, seeds... Come, I'm going to smurf you some seeds.

Here's a good spot. Smurf me a sack.

You don't have anything bigger?

Uh... no.

You could use your hat.

Take off my hat? So you can see my smurf? No way!

→PFFFT!←

Hee! Hee!

There are plenty to choose from. Shall I smurf you a little of everything?

BZZZz

BUZZz

Come on, go away.

Go away, I said!

BZ?

THAT'S ENOUGH! SMURF ME ALONE!

BZZZZZZzzz

CLACK!

ZZZZ

THANKS FOR THE ADVICE!

BZZZZZZZZZ

Very angry he is.

Run you should.

For smurfs' sake! That bumblebee won't give up!

Bzzzzz

zzzzz

BZZZZzzz²

!

SPLASH

BZZZHEEHEEHEEHEE

Do you want us to smurf seeds from these?

Yes, please!

Weird plants. You sure they aren't poisonous?

No, not at all!

!?

But only in wet meadows they grow...

And very, very heavy you are!

SPLOTCH

23

27

Farther up the river...

You still don't smurf anything?

No, Papa Smurf. No trace of them, nor their boat.

We have to land. The waterfall isn't far.

THE WATERFALL!

If the wave smurfed them to here, it would be a catasmurfre. We have to go look.

Let's keep going on foot. We'll smurf past the rocks!

This time, we have to get smurfing.

I understand. We don't want to take advantage of your good nature!

May I smurf a little trumpet-call of farewell?

WE'RE LEAVING!

Farewell!

Delighted to have met you!

Thank you for everything! A nice trip back we wish to you!

Pilus, help! In Pilulit, disaster has struck!

Huh? What disaster?

!

PIF

AAAAAAH!

BIG BLUE MONSTERS!

Whoa there! Let's be polite!

Fear you must not have! Very nice the Smurfs are! But in Pilulit what's happening?

Our city other monsters have invaded!

Even more awful than these they are!

A tunnel under the big gate they dug...

At night from their hole they came out and our supplies devoured! And our houses to enter they're trying!

What do they look like, your monsters?

Round ears they have!

And long teeth like this!

Very big and hairy they are!

Like huge earthworms their tails look!

Without a doubt, they're rats!

Poor Pilus! Rats can be smurfly nasty!

We're really sorry to leave you after this bad news!

Trust in us you can have! Bravely we will fight!

25

29

Brother Pilus to Pilulit return we must! Our parents, companions, and children defend we must!

Oh, really? They have families?

Alas, harvest and tools abandon we must! Our march they'll slow!

WHAT?! All our seeds?

For nothing we worked!

It's really sad for them!

Yes! It smurfs my heart!

Hey, we can't smurf them like this!

But we have to go back!

Yes, but it's an emergency--

We have to smurf something!

I agree!

If you'd like, we'll smurf to Pilulit with you!

We'll bring your harvest and smurf these rats a lesson!

What?! Seriously you speak?

Hurrah! Long live the Smurfs!

Long live our heroes!

With you, Pilulit we'll save!

Quick! Let's find some strong leaves to smurf into bundles!

Smurf your seeds onto these!

And your tools here!

There! Everything's smurfed! Let's go!

26

Is Pilulit very far?

For you, no! Big steps you can make!

We can smurf to the bottom of the waterfall over here!

Not so fast or I'll smurf a leg! I'm... uh... 500 and some odd years old, still and all!

No pieces of their boat... The river must have smurfed them far away!

Here, Papa Smurf! Some tracks of footsteps!

They're everywhere... There are lots of them!

I hope they're safe and smurf!

They smurfed this way!

They lit some tiny fires! Weird!

And they smurfed a shelter over there!

For smurfness sake, if they didn't drown,

WHERE DID THEY GO?!

→Pffft!← It isn't very far but it's smurfly high!

Yes! In the mountains our city is nestled!

Night is going to smurf... We can't keep going very long!

You're right! Until sunrise we should camp!

27

31

You mentioned your companions... So are there girls, Pilus?

No! **PILIS** they're called!

And do Pilis look like you?

Well, special they are!

All the time makeup they put on and their they hair do!

And about their clothing they talk!

You Pilus never do your hair?

Well... no! Do you?

Hmm! Enough smurfing! It's time to sleep!

I hope no victims of these rats there have been!

Oh, very cautious everyone is!

Yes! Locked inside their homes they'll stay!

The next day, finally...

Here we are! In the midst of the boulders our city is built!

Only through this narrow pass we can enter!

There's no denying it's smurfy well hidden!

Do we really have to smurf through there?

It's creepy!

Whoa! It's getting narrower and narrower! I'm afraid of getting smurfed!

We told you to watch your waistline, Greedy Smurf!

Behind this gate Pilulit is!

Through here the monsters entered!

Under the gate they dug!

I wonder how the rats smurfed their way here...

Some seeds we must have dropped! And the path they followed!

The Pilus gatekeepers I must call!

PWAAAP

Hey! Not bad! What smurfing tone!

Well? At their post they are not!

As I said, in their homes they all hid away!

Wait, I will smurf you a helping hand!

GNNNNNN!

There! Go ahead!

To Pilulit welcome!

WOOW!
Impressive! It takes my smurf away!

Watch out! In that tunnel the monsters are hiding!

I don't think they'll smurf from there before nighttime!

You'll see! Well protected we are! But nothing here grows! Just moss and some mushrooms!

Since lots of gray us surrounds us, the walls we decorate!

Ah, yes, it's... uh... original!

Wait! These mushrooms look like they're good to smurf!

Mmmph... Shucculent!

Yuck!

Ugh!

DISGUSTING BIG PERSON HE IS! A MUSHROOM HE ATE!

Hey, shorty! Smurf it out or I'll treat myself to a Pilus fritter!

Look! The storehouse gate the monsters smashed and all our seed they ate!

HEY, PILUS! BACK WE ARE!

CRRREEEEE

AAAAAH! BLUE GIANTS!

Fear you must not have! To help us our friends the Smurfs have come! Very nice they are!

Nice, them?! Are you kidding us?

Not at all! Without fear you can come out!

Uh... Hello, everyone!

31

35

To the Elected Pilus I must speak!

In the Council Chamber they are! Ever since the beasts came, an emergency meeting they've been holding!

To the tenth floor I climb! Our Elected Pilus I will see!

What's a LectedPilus?

ELECTED PILUS we said!

Every three years, three Pilus we elect the city to lead!

Well, drat! We just have a Papa Smurf and we never change! I think their system is smurfly advanced!

That remains to be seen! Wait...

Say... Can Pilis be elected, too?!

Elected Pilis? Of course not!

Ha! Ha! Funny ideas you have!

You see? Not all that advanced!

Honorable... ahhh... Elected Pilus... ⇒pfff...⇐ I greet you!

Ah, PiluPen! You're finally here!

A tragedy we've experienced!

Everything will work out! Powerful allies I've brought, the Smurfs!

The what?

Come...from the balcony you'll see them!

OH! WHOA PILUS!

Huge they are!

Creatures like them we've never seen!

36

PiluPen, a big risk you took! To our city giant strangers you invited. Our sovereignty they threatened!

But tonight, the rats will come out and our new harvest devour! To chase them off the Smurfs we need! Hmm... Right you are! An exception we could make!

But in this case a resolution we must draw up! Yes, hard work awaits us! When we've finished, let you know we will!

The Elected Pilus always things complicate!

My friends, the Smurfs will protect us! Until nightfall, your regular activities you can resume!

The Elected Pilus declaration we must wait for! The city I will show you!

Hey... Do the Elected Pilus have special abilities? Oh, yes! The first, great jokes they tell!

The second, the reed pipe beautifully plays and the third, his ears can wiggle!

But... That doesn't smurf anything about leading the city! Uh... No, but a choice had to be made!

I'm impressed! It takes courage for these tiny Pilus to smurf all these homes!

33

It's smurfy all over!

Say, you should smurf a look inside! It's very comfortable!

Oh, yes?

EEEEEEEK!

Oh, sorry, uh... Miss!

Look... Here the Pilis the harvest are dealing with! The seeds they must sort, clean, dry...

And sometimes even grind!

But then, the Pilis work a lot! I thought they smurfed all their time styling their hair and chatting?

WHAT?! WHO SAID THAT?!

Uh... Not me, in any case!

Here's the school for the little Pilus who we call Lil'Pilus! Here Botany and Pilus grammar they learn!

No one's there! Is that because of the rats?

During the summer months, on vacation the Lil'Pilus are!

34

In this pool, the Pilis their laundry come to wash!

HOLD ON THERE!

SPLASH

Oh, the rascals! All drenched I am!

Bad seed! Run off and play elsewhere!

Hee! Hee! Hee!

For the hundredth time, into the washing pool you can't jump!

Being naughty you must stop! The wall go paint!

Always the wall to paint we must!

A pain the oldsters are!

In this area the elderly get together. Harvesting they no longer do!

I understand. They're no longer able to smurf work anymore!

Oh, they can...

But they no longer want to!

Should I shoot or should I point?

Uh... Hello, everyone!

It feels like they don't trust us! We must try to smurf to know them!

Thash true!

Ah, there's PiluPat! Hey, would you introduce us to your friends?

I'm PiluPaul! Color you don't see well?

->Pfft!<- The most smurfing thing with these Pilus is they all look alike!

Really impressive they are!

Really handsome I think they are! Hee! Hee! Hee!

HANDSOME?! These big hairless blues?

Phooey! Whatever!

What about you, PiluPen? Do you have a companion? You've already smurfed a family?

No! With my parents I still live. A problem of housing...

Housing?

Yes! To be able to marry, a new cave each Pilu must dig!

HOOOONK

Ah! The Elected Pilus are coming to speak!

Uh... By virtue of the powers from the Pilus people in us invested, the following proclamation we make...

As a special case, the temporary presence in our city of a contingent of blue giants we authorize! The protection of the community they will insure and the invaders by all means necessary will expel!

Then, in turn, as soon as possible, our land they will leave! Thus have we decided! Long live the Pilus! Long live Pilulit!

A nice declaration we wrote!

And only three hours it took!

As usual, the situation perfectly we're managing!

Bravo! The rats to fight you're authorized!

Oh, yeah? ‑>GULP!‑<

Frankly, that puts us in a fine smurf!

Maybe we smurfed a little quickly... Rats are big! And nasty!

I don't want to get smurfed!

Oh, no! We smurfed our word! We have to keep it!

Here's what I propose: tonight we hide! We wait until the rats come out to smurf the seeds...

And then, **BAM!** We leap in front of them and smurf the living day-lights out of them!

Oh, yes? You think it's as scary as all that?

Greedy Smurf's right. We can't smurf the rats barehanded! We need weapons!

To work! I'm missing some tools, but I'll smurf with what I can find!

Night fell over Pilulit.
In the city, nothing stirred...

Suddenly...

Look out, they're here! Forward!

Ahem... They aren't running away much...

Then let's go! One... Two...

THREE! ATTACK!

HIYAAAH!

Uh...

PFFFRT! KSSS!

PONNNN

Well played, Harmony Smurf!

For once!

Hurrah!

Victory!

Long live the Smurfs!

The beasts they drove off!

Fantastic! Great heroes you are!

Well, it's not the first time!

This great victory we must celebrate!

Good idea! Your instruments go get!

And there they go! They're at it again!

Anyway, the rats won't smurf out of their hole anymore tonight!

That's for sure!

Yes, but tomorrow? They're sure to come back! And we can't smurf here forever!

That's right! I'm tired of smurfing seeds and mushrooms!

I might have an idea... I need to smurf a word with PiluPen...

PONNNN

TOOOOT

PON?

PLEASE, QUIET!

The rats for good chased away must be! And ourselves we can do it! But lots of courage we will need!

Speak, PiluPen!

For Pilulit we will fight!

The next morning, a strange army got ready...

Everyone is here?

Yes, PiluPen!

Brave Pilus, on you we count!

Our city you must free!

With all our hearts we cheer you!

Courage! You're going to smurf a decisive victory!

My friends, forward!

40

44

PLAN
PLAN
RATAPLAN

For Pilulit...
**ALL
TOGETHER!**

PLAN
PLAN

POOOT
PON

POOOT
PON

TOOOOT

PWAAAP

PON
PLAN

They must be at the bottom!
We can't smurf anything
more to help them there!

POOOOT
POOOT

Quick,
to the
gate!

Well?

Still
nothing!

Poor Pilus!
I hope I didn't
get them
smurfed!

THEY DID IT!
The rats are smurfing
at full speed!

HOORAY!

PON
POOOOT

POOOOT

PON

PLAN
PLAN

Saved we are!

For our valiant Pilus, HURRAH!

Bravo! You chased them away all by yourselves, like big people!

If they come back one day, you can just smurf the same thing!

While we're waiting, we can fill their tunnel back up!

You're right! I'll go smurf some big stones!

Leave it! This job I'll handle!

?

Him? But...

Yes, yes, trust him you can!

These rockets for our celebrations we use!

Get back, quick!

BOOM POOM BROOM

42

There, it's filled back in! Hee! Hee! Hee!

For smurfs' sake! These Pilus always surprise me!

And now, a very, very big celebration we will have!

AH, NO! NO WAY!

I mean... We must smurf on our way without delay!

ONE MOMENT!

To thank you, from the tenth floor we have come down! Very grateful we are! You saved us!

Yes! Pilus you deserve to be!

Farewell, everyone!

Smurf good care of yourselves!

Please... Where Pilulit is no one tell!

Of course! We don't want our village to be smurfed, either!

So long, goodbye!

Dang Pilus! I'm going to miss them!

Yes, but not their cooking!

Nor their music!

Let's go! If at a good pace we smurf, in our village before night we'll arrive!

Oops! It was time to leave! I'm beginning to smurf like the Pilus!

Let's smurf the lessons from this adventure... True greatness is what's inside! Someone brave and small is worth more than a smurf who's all big! A big mind can live in a small body and, as Papa Smurf always says...

Uh-oh! The return trip is going to feel smurfly long!

In the village...

I don't understand where they could have smurfed! It's a real mystery!

Papa Smurf, about our missing folks... I've got an idea to smurf you!

Oh, yes? I'm listening, Sculptor Smurf!

Here! I smurfed this drawing for a monument in their memory...

But what are you smurfing me with your monument! They'll be back eventually!

Oh? You think so?

Okay, okay, fine! I'll go smurf it in my drawer...

There's our forest! I'll be really happy to smurf home!

Still, I'm going to miss feeling big and strong!

Yes, you get used to that quickly!

I definitely had no luck fishing! Lentils for dinner, as usual!

OH!

AAAH!

Rather, it'll be
A SMURF KEBAB!

We're no longer giants for sure!

SMURF FOR YOUR LIVES!

End of The Smurfs Journey to Pilulit

Oh, yes? It ends like that?!

What a story! I wonder where he smurfed all those ideas!

OWIE! I didn't see the time smurf while I was reading! I'm all numb!

Brainy Smurf?

Hey, Brainy Smurf!

I'M HERE!

I finally found you! So did you read my book?

Uh... Yes, I smurfed a look!

You smurfed a big job! But frankly, your story is too implausible! And it smurfs all over the place!

Oh?

Plus you smurfed us in far-fetched roles! I seem like a moralizing pest!

Oh, surely not!

And Gargamel? He smurfed their path right on the last page, as if by chance! It's really too smurf a gesture!

Hmmph!

But I don't want to discourage you! Some less demanding Smurfs may like your book! Like Jokey Smurf... Or Dopey Smurf!

Yes, okay, I understand! Smurf me my manuscript!

It's there, at the foot of the tree!

?

CLIP-CLOP CLIP-CLOP

45

49

Another clearing! I'm completely lost in this forest! I should've brought my guide book to roads, routes, and castles...

I'll give you a breather for a minute and then we'll go! We have to get to Garlic Castle before night!

Hey? What's this?

A tiny book filled with strange words! It looks like a novel...

I'll try to decipher it! Maybe I could use the story...

If not, I'll get a few coins for it from a curio dealer! Come on, Gulliver! Let's hit the road!

I'm a poor solitary minstrel, far, far away from his home... ♪♫

My manuscript! He took my manuscript!

Well, you'll smurf another! Maybe it will be more successful than that one!

THE ADVENTURES OF BENNY BREAKIRON

PAR PEYO
ET Blesteau

THE MAGIC DOLL

...And our big show will end with that, Ladies and Gentlemen! Good night and see you again soon!

That's it! Another successful evening, right, Augustus?

For sure, Mister Bodoni!

Are you Mister Bodoni, the director of this circus?

Ah! Let me tell you how much I enjoyed your show! What astonishing precision! What quality! So much effort and work, this all must be showcased!

You're too kind, I--

But tell me, didn't you have a number with a very, very strong young boy...? His name is escaping me...

Ah, Benny! Benny Breakiron!

That's it! What's become of him?

He left us after saving us from bankruptcy! But he still writes to us from time to time.

Ah? So, you have his address then?

I have his letters in my trailer. Come, I'll show them to you!

This is charming! And what lovely handwriting!

Isn't it? A drop of port?

Gladly! Between you and me, that young Benny's strength wasn't real, was it? How do I put it... Was he playing a trick?

Absolutely not! He was a veritable Hercules!

But a Hercules with an Achilles heel! Whenever he catches a cold, he loses all his strength!

That's so weird! And I see that he lives in Vi... Vivejoie-la-Grande!

What the heck is that Madame Demonia doing in there? The show's been over for more than an hour!

Madame Demonia knows what she's doing... Besides, there she is!

It's about time!

Is everything all right, Madame Demonia?

Everything's fine. Let's go!

And where to, Madame?

To Vivejoie-la-Grande!

2

Vivejoie-la-Grande, Sunday morning...

Benny Breakiron is a little boy just like all the other little boys his age...

...with one tiny little difference, however.

BEEEP BEEP

SCREEEEEER

What's going on?

Hey, get moving! You p...

Go fly a k...

And you, you loser of a--

You took your driving test in...

Dang!

Are you going to back up or what, you country bumpkin? You can see we can't get by!

Back up yourself, nitwit!

Of course! It's a bus of people from Hicksville!

Those Roco people don't obey rules!

I should help them! What if I...?

The difference with other little boys...

...is that Benny is strong!...

3

55

...UNBELIEVABLY STRONG!

And voilà*!

Sometimes, it's fun being really strong because then you can help people!

What happened?

...I ...I don't know!

We don't care, get going!

Did you see? It's him!

Incredible!

We need him. Follow him!

I'm going to go by Jules Petty Square to see if my friends are there!

Huh? What the--?

I've got him! Hit it!

*French for "There."

56

Hello, Benny! I'm delighted to meet you!

? ?

But... uh... Hello, Ma'am. What is this...?

My name is Demonia, and I'm a good friend of Bodoni--

MONSIEUR* BODONI, YOU KNOW HIM?

For a long time now! I saw him again last night, and he told me you certainly wouldn't refuse to do me a little favor...

Of course! What is it?

Oh! Nothing much! But I'll explain it to you at the castle.

If you agree, you won't regret it! You'll be able to pay for your candy till the end of your life! Do you smoke?...

Shut up, idiot!

POW

?

What did that man mean?

Nothing, nothing!

Ah, we're here!

Zlip! What are you waiting for? Go open the gate!

Yeah! I'll do that!

5

*French for "Mister."

What weather! Come inside quickly, young Benny!

Lousy country ☆◎✦⚡

I can't wait till we pull this job and make off with the dough to go tan in the sunshine!

Shut up, Zlip!

Take your things off, dear child.

Thanks, but I'd rather keep my scarf on! It's not very warm in your home, and I'm afraid of catching a cold! And whenever I catch I cold, I--

You're absolutely right!... So, Zlip, get a fire going in the hearth.

Okay! I'll get you a darn nice fire burning in no time at all.

Zlip! Please! Your language!

That boy is impossible! And yet, he owes me everything! I pulled him out of the gutter!

GLUG GLUG GLUG

Come sit down beside me, and let's chat!

SCRATCH

WHAM

Will that do?

?

Moron! You're going to ruin everything!

Oh, Molleton, shut up, you!

⑥

58

Do you want something to drink? A little barley water?

Well, uh... I would!

Barley water? Jee whiz, Madame Demonia, this kid isn't a toddler anymore!

I'm going to make him a nice Irish coffee!*

What's that Irish coffee thingy?

Hmm!... It's... It's very good! You'll see!

But let's get to the point! Here goes! At the moment, there's a big exhibition of treasures of African art at the museum.

Oh, yes! We had a school fieldtrip to visit it. There are terrible, scary things in it!

They said thieves have tried to get into the museum, but they haven't succeeded. I think it's well guarded, isn't it?

Hmmm... Indeed! So, in--

WHAM

Okay! Here's your barley water!

So, in that exhibition, there's a little object of no value I'd very much like to have.

SSNIF!S

Alas! The curator absolutely refuses to sell it to me, so we thought of you...

Yeah! You're strong! So you could bust through the doors, knock out the guards, and swipe the thingamajig!... What do you think about that?

?

BUT... BUT THAT WOULD BE **STEALING!**

7

*Irish coffee is made of coffee, Irish whiskey, sugar and cream. It is illegal to serve alcohol to minors.

Oh! Stealing, stealing...

Why, not at all! Furthermore, Article 24, Paragraph 2A, Subparagraph 12, of the peddybourgeois penal code says this... Listen...

No! I'm not listening to you! You're crooks! I'd rather leave!

No way, snotnose! You're going nowhere!

Really?

POW
KRAK

Careful, little guy! That could cause you problems!

You're the one who is going to have some! I'm going to call the police!

Give me that phone or I'll get mad!

CLANG

Hello?...

BAM BAM

AH HAAA!

HEY!

BLAF

Assault and battery and property damage! That's for starters!

Hello... Line 22 in Asnières?

Calm down, Benny! There's no use fighting me! I'm the strongest, and you're going to do as I say! Look deep into my eyes! Deep...

8

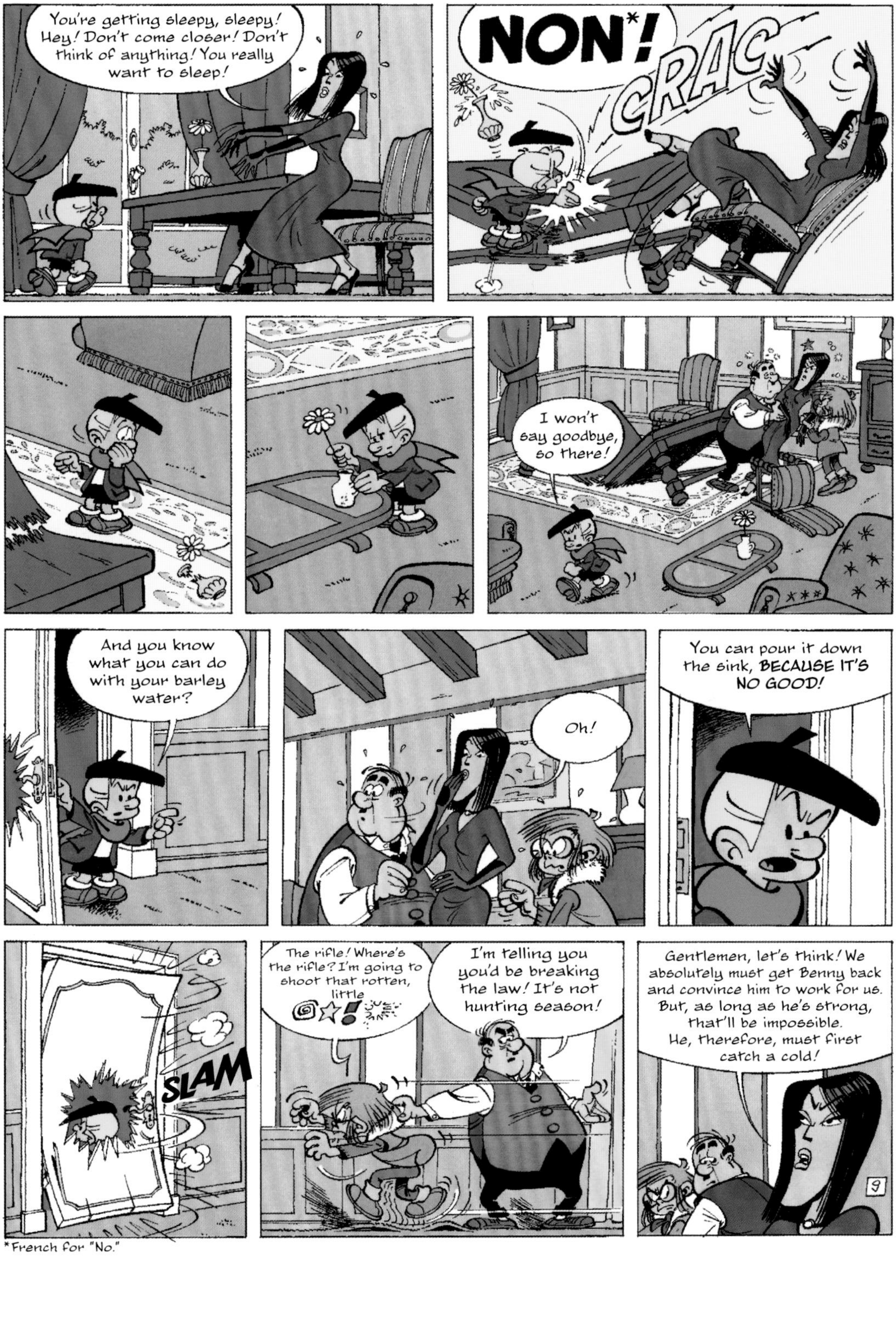
You're getting sleepy, sleepy! Hey! Don't come closer! Don't think of anything! You really want to sleep!
NON*!
CRAC
I won't say goodbye, so there!
And you know what you can do with your barley water?
Oh!
You can pour it down the sink, BECAUSE IT'S NO GOOD!
SLAM
The rifle! Where's the rifle? I'm going to shoot that rotten, little
I'm telling you you'd be breaking the law! It's not hunting season!
Gentlemen, let's think! We absolutely must get Benny back and convince him to work for us. But, as long as he's strong, that'll be impossible. He, therefore, must first catch a cold!
9

*French for "No."

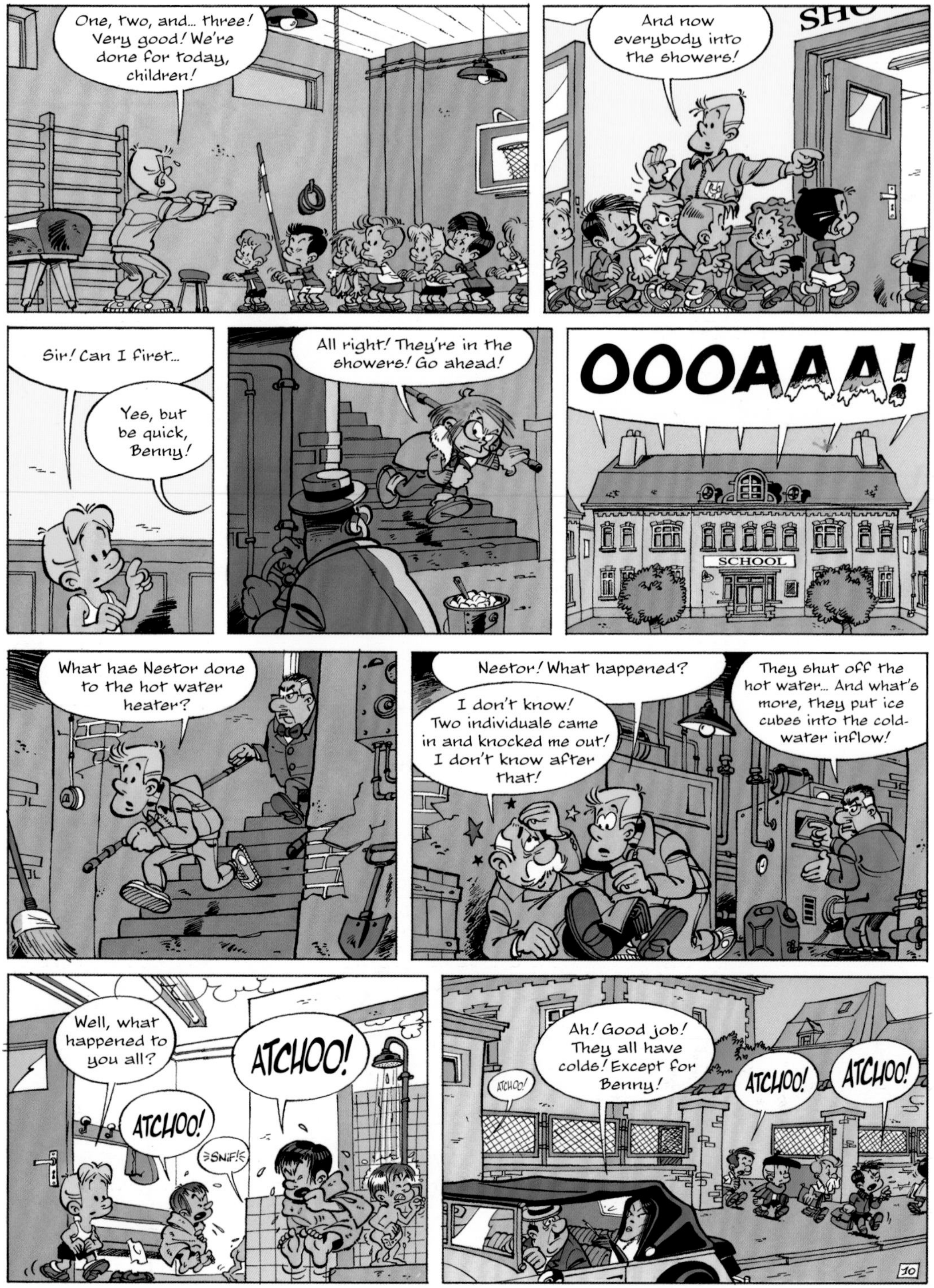
One, two, and... three! Very good! We're done for today, children!
SHO
And now everybody into the showers!
Sir! Can I first...
Yes, but be quick, Benny!
All right! They're in the showers! Go ahead!
OOOAAA!
SCHOOL
What has Nestor done to the hot water heater?
Nestor! What happened?
I don't know! Two individuals came in and knocked me out! I don't know after that!
They shut off the hot water... And what's more, they put ice cubes into the cold-water inflow!
Well, what happened to you all?
ATCHOO!
ATCHOO!
SNIF!
ATCHOO!
Ah! Good job! They all have colds! Except for Benny!
ATCHOO!
ATCHOO!
10

That afternoon, at the Jules Petty Square...

...and then they asked me to steal an object from the African art exhibition. I swear to you it's true!

Oh, stop your storytelling and play!

A LA BELLA CASSATA! VANILLA! CHOCOLATA! RASPBERRIA!

Do you have pistachio?

Vanilla and raspberry for me!

I don't have any money!

That's okay, I have some!

Hey! Dere! Did yoo a-see de beautiful, little bird-a?...

OH! PARDONNA!

PLOP

Whoa! Oooh! That's cold!

Scusi! Ba I no do dat deliberately!

Yes, you did! I saw you, child-torturer!

?

Torturer of bambino? Me? Ba look what's in dere first before accoosing me!

Well, what? It's ice cream!

Yeah! And put a lid on it!

BAM

Wait! We'll help you, Mister guard!

ᴤBRR!ᴥ I'll be lucky if I don't catch a cold after that!

Demonia can't say anymore that Zlip doesn't have good ideas! Heh heh!

Excellent idea, Zlip! See the result: nothing!

But, Madame Demonia, I--

Wait! I see our chance to soak him good! You never know... Hold up! I'm stepping on it!

Why, that's Madame Demonia's car! Well, those people could pay attention where they're driving! I'm drenched!

Hello, Mme* Minou!

Benny! But you're all wet! Come quick and dry off!

What's that huge package?

Ah, yes! I don't know! A truck brought it for you! They said it was a gift!

But... it's a bale of hay?!

Hay! Oh, my! And I'm allergic to... AAA--AAA--

--CHOOO!

There! I threw the hay onto the vacant lot! I'm sorry!

It's okay, it'll pass!

Good night, Mme Minou!

SNT

Your hay idea was excellent, Madame Demonia! Result: his landlady was the one who's got a cold!

Oh! Spare me your sarcasm, Zlip! Go get me this instead! We'll succeed tonight!

His bedroom window is the first one on the left on the second floor! Do you have the dry ice? Good! Then, go ahead!

12

*Mme is short for Madame.

The next morning, at the moment when the sun casts its first rays over Vivejoie-la-Grande...

ATCHOO!

Did you hear?

Yeah! Hahaaa! That's it! We've got him!

Gentlemen! Let's go!

Bless you, Mme Minou!

Thanks, that's-- Why... why, your room is full of snow!

Yeah! There are no seasons anymore, are there?

HA HA HA! We've got you! You've got your cold!

A cold? Not at all!

Don't lie to me! We heard you sneezing!

That's not me. That's Mme Minou!

But... but then you're still very strong?

YES!

POW

POW

Yes, they are bandits, Mme Minou! They want me to catch a cold to steal something at the museum and--

Yes, Benny! ⇒Sniff...⇐ Drink your chocolate while it's hot and afterwards, you ⇒sniff...⇐ you'll go tell those two gentlemen you're sorry!

Say, Madame Demonia, what if we gave up?

Absolutely not! A few days ago, I read an article in a medical journal! And that article is giving me an idea... Mr. Molleton, drive us to the Postur Institute!

65

The Postur Institute, a center acclaimed for its bacteriological research...

So, Bert? How's your work going?

Making progress!

Look, I've already managed to isolate the cold virus!

Are you sure of that, my dear colleague?

Yes, my dear colleague. Yes, I'm sure of that! Why do you ask me that, dear colleague?

Oh! No reason, dear colleague, but since you made a tiny little mistake last time -- "Errare humanum est*" -- you'll tell me, I was wondering if--

No, dear colleague, I didn't make any mistakes this time. And if you want proof, have a good whiff of this!

No! Don't uncork that test tube! That's dangerous!

ATCHOOO!

Good job, Bert. You've done it!

Thanks! Now I have to find the anti-- antido-- A... AAAAH...

ATCHOO!

ATCHOO!

Gesundheit**! Atchooo! That test tube...

≥SNIF!≤

You're going to give us that test tube!

Yeah! And quick, or else bang bang and no more atchoos!

! ?

*Latin for "To err is human."   **German for "Bless you" or "Health."

66

Five airmail stamps and a lottery ticket for Mme Minou...

There he is! He's going into the post office! Go ahead, Molleton!

Darn! Lots of people!

Window #8...

It's the third time I've been here!

But, Ma'am, I was ahead of you!

And my soup is on the stove!

Ah! And we're the ones paying for these postal workers!

CLANG

Ew! What is that?

Don't panic! Another one of those scruffy kids threw a stink bomb! Open the windows!

It doesn't smell so bad! But I... AAA... AAA... AAA...

Ah! Young people!

≷SNIF!≷

TCHAAAATCHOOOO

I'm sure that was them again!

ATCHOO!

My hat!

My pension!

ATCHOOO!

Close the windows!

My check!

My deposit!

My rubber check!

ACHRAM!

Too late!

Quick!

The pharmacy!

ME, SICK!

!

And I still don't have a cold!

KROINc

Oh! My goodness!

Five airmail stamps and one lottery ticket.

ATCHOOO!

!

Get in line like everyone!

PHARMACY

And my soup is still on the stove!

No pushing in back!

My antibiotics for two tubes of flu meds.

Deal!

Crook!

But, Ma'am, I was in front of you!

They've gone too far this time! I'm going to tell the police!

16

POLICE STATION

Atchoo!

Atchoo!

Goodness, bless you! Want it wrapped?

It's not fro--atchoo--zen, I hope?

Bless you!

TCHOO!

Good heavens! Why, of course!

Raised on hormones, seven letters, it's c.h.i.c.k.e.n...

NOK NOK

Come in!

Chief, young Benny Breakiron is here!

Him again! Okay, send him in and bring me an aspirin!

Well?

So, here goes...

...And Zlip shut off the hot water at school because they wanted me to catch a cold to force me to steal at the museum, which I didn't want to do, and so they made me drink barley water that's no good, and then everyone caught a cold at the post office and--

PENAL CODE

Okay, okay! I'll see what I can do!

Yes, but be quick because they're dangerous! They even made it snow in my bedroom, not to mention the bale of hay that--

Whatever!

ATCHOOO!

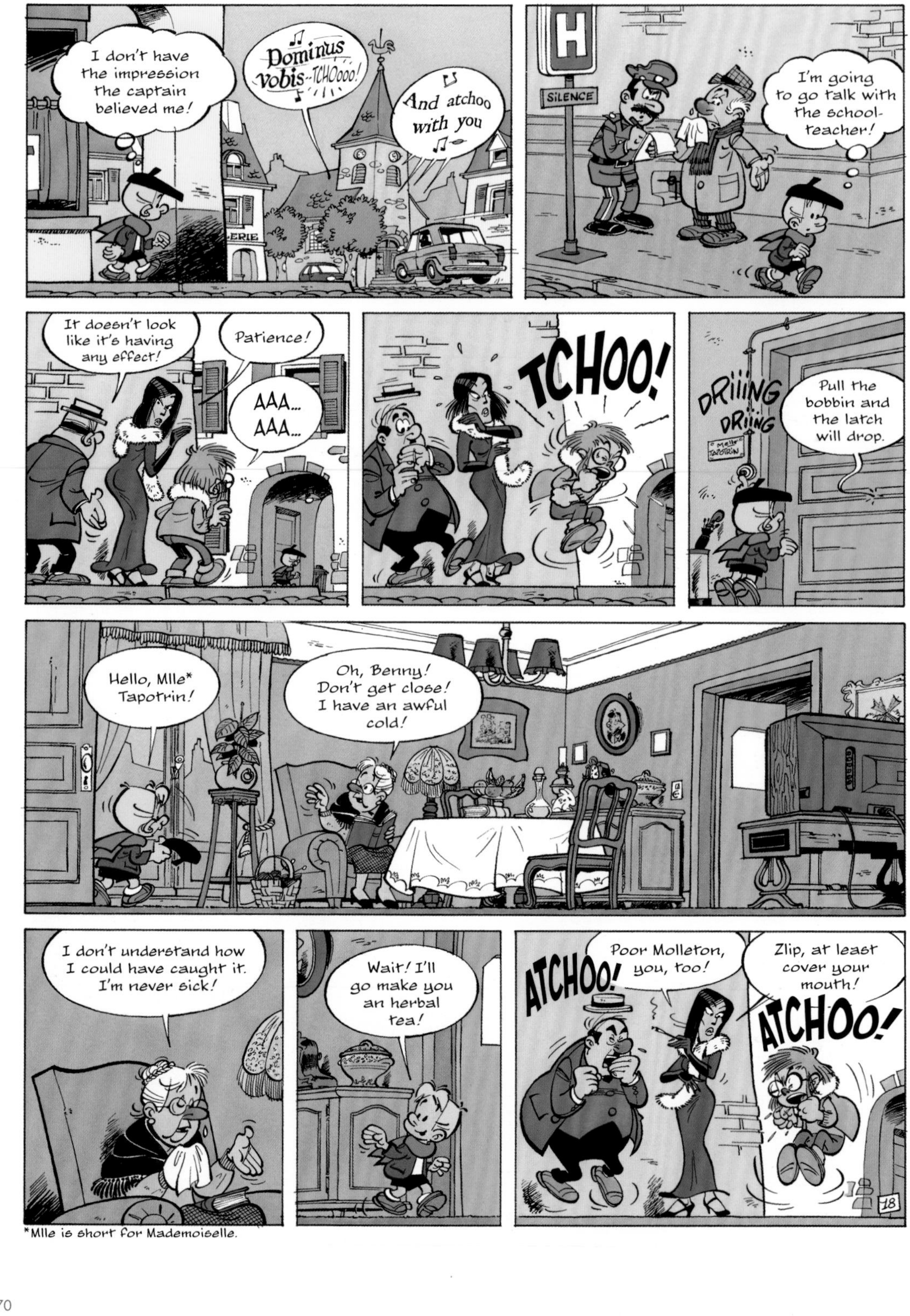
I don't have the impression the captain believed me!
Dominus vobis-TCHOooo!
And atchoo with you
SILENCE
I'm going to go talk with the school-teacher!
It doesn't look like it's having any effect!
Patience!
AAA... AAA...
TCHOO!
DRIIING DRIING
Mlle TAPOTRIN
Pull the bobbin and the latch will drop.
Hello, Mlle* Tapotrin!
Oh, Benny! Don't get close! I have an awful cold!
I don't understand how I could have caught it. I'm never sick!
Wait! I'll go make you an herbal tea!
ATCHOO!
Poor Molleton, you, too!
Zlip, at least cover your mouth!
ATCHOO!
18

*Mlle is short for Mademoiselle.

Benny, could you turn on the TV? It's time for the news!

...and following that hunting expedition, it was finally possible to sign the disarmament accords...

...In Vivejoie-la-Grande, a cold--ATCHOOO!... epidemic is breaking out at the moment...

...The research department of the Postur Institute is making every effort to ease that epidemic... Atchooo!

ATCHOOO!

Bless you!

We have--ATCHOOO! The situation--ATCHOOO! ...well in hand... →SMRFFF...←

The mayor declared to us:

ATCHOOO!

What the heck is he doing?

Here's your herbal tea!

Thank you! Oh! I don't usually do this, but for once, I'd gladly add a tiny drop of rum.

The bottle is in that armoire.

Here?

!

19

71

Hee hee hee! You don't recognize him? That's Alphonso! The skeleton from the science classes!

Oh, yeah! Hi, Alphonso.

Here's your bottle!

I'll come by tomorrow! Take good care of yourself, Mlle Tapotrin!

Thanks, Benny! And you be good!

⸙Brrr...⸙ That Alphonso! I know he's made of plastic, but he still sends shivers down my spine!

ATCHOOO!

Yippee!

That's it!

ATCHOOO!

And now you're going to do what we say! And you'll go take that object from the museum!

I'm glad to. But now that I have a cold, I'm a little boy like all the rest!

! ! !

20

Good heavens, but it's true! When he has a cold, he loses all his strength!

Why, then it's all no use!

Let's not panic. To start with, Zlip, lock him in the little bedroom!

Okay. Come on, you rotten kid!

ATCHOOO!

CLIC

I can see only one solution: we have to cure his cold ASAP!

Think, Molleton! If he's cured, he'll get his strength back. We must find a way to convince him to do what we say before then!

Okay, but what?

I think I've got it! Zlip, go get my first aid kit!

Wait for me. I'm going up to old Bradstone's room.

?

Hello, Colonel Bradstone.

Hi! Are you bringing me my whiskey?

No. I've come to give you your little shot.

My shot? But you already gave me one yesterday!

Come, come. Stay calm, and I'll bring you your whiskey!

Molleton! Zlip! Go find me Benny.

I wonder what she did to the old man?

Don't ask questions, Zlip. We have to trust Madame Demonia!

All right, come on, kid!

Where are you taking me?

Don't ask questions. We must trust Madame Demonia!

Poor Colonel Bradstone!

AGAAAa

FLEBELEB

TUT

?

?

?

TCHOOF
TCHOOF
♪

Who's that man? What's wrong with him?

He's my uncle, a former colonial doctor who, during his last trip to Africa, was bewitched by a witch doctor from the tribe in which my uncle was working!

FFRRRT

Nothing but a small magic doll, which at this moment is at the museum, can break the spell... Alas! I couldn't get it!

And the exhibition is leaving in a few days and, if I don't get that magic doll, the old... uh, my uncle is doomed!

I asked you to commit that theft in order to put an end to this poor man's awful suffering!

There! I've told you the truth! Now, my beloved uncle's recovery depends entirely on you!

Act according to your conscience! Whatever you do, I won't be angry. Go! You're free!

But... but why didn't you tell me all that?

≡SNIF!≡

Under those conditions, I obviously agree to help you!

POW!

Heeheehee

Unfortunately, so long as I have my cold, I won't be able to do anything!

23

≠SNIF!≠

If only there were a cure to get rid of my cold right away!

A cure!

The laboratory!

Scientists!

Antidote!

Let's go!

ATCHOOO!

Here, Colonel. Here's your whiskey!

Scotch? Yum yum!

Hi! It's us again!

Hello!

Excuse us, but it's for the Colonel who needs a magic doll in the museum because he's sick so you have to cure my cold really, really fast because it's going to close!

But... we've been looking for three years and haven't–..

Well then, we'll give you three minutes to do so or else...

Hand me the methyl salicylamide.

With the polyvidone, don't you think?

No!

Uh... Here! Try drinking this.

Are you sure that...?

Uh...

24

Yuck!

GLUG
GLUG
GLUG

ATCHHHOOO!

We found it! The cold is at its peak!

We just have to reverse the process then!

I doubt it!

There. Three drops in your nose.

I don't believe so!

Well?

I don't know. Wait...

≋SNiF!≋

I'd be surprised!

?! POW

Yippee! My cold is cured! I've got my strength back! We can go!

Bravo, dear colleague. Quick! Let's note down our miraculous formula!

Agreed! Which base did you use?

Well, I don't really know anymore! Phenacetin or polyvidone?

I think I added propyl, no, uh...

Unless...

Go to the museum, Molleton, step on it!

25

Here! This is the map of the museum. Here's the photo of the magic doll. It's in the "L" room. Take this flashlight and good luck!

Hey, kid, the guards are armed. So, just in case, taken this Tommy gun. It may prove useful to you!

Thanks, Monsieur Zlip! So, I just have to push on the trigger like this and--

Hey! Careful! It's loaded! It's--it's dangerous!

If it's dangerous, you keep it then. Okay, I'm going!

How do you plan to get in?

Well, I'll simply bust down that stupid door!

NO!

Don't do that! The slightest contact with that door will automatically set off an alarm that'll alert the guards! We know something about that!

Okay. In that case, we must find another solution! And I can see only one!

?

! !

26

78

Zut*!
It's locked from inside!

Quietly...
Quietly...
CRO ......

No alarm?
Okay, I'm going in!

The door!
Where's the door?

Ah! There it is.

Let's see. Where am I on here? Stairs "A," "B," or "C"! And in which building?

AND BANG AND POW!
I SHOOT DOWN THE FIRST ONE I SEE!

*French interjection, similar to "Heck!" or "Drat!"

And after we won, as a reward for my heroic conduct, I was named corporal!

Well, goodness me, Mr. Lagloriole, without you we maybe would have lost that war!

You're telling me, kid!

I can honestly say I saved the country!

~Whew!~

Okay. Room "L"?

ROOM Q

RESTROOMS

Zut! I'm completely lost!

Ah! There's someone.

Z

Pardon me, sir. Room "L," please.

Huh? What? ~Hic!~... Room "L"? One... one moment!

You go down the big stairs, and it's immediately to the left.

Z SNR

Thanks!

HEY! GOOD GRACIOUS! COME HERE A SEC!

I hope everything is going well!

28

You wouldn't want to pass me the... ⇒Hic...⇐ bottle... there, in the corner?

Do you want a little glass?

No thanks!

Besides, Mlle Tapotrin, the schoolteacher always says drinking is bad for your health, that whoever has drunk will drink, and when parents drink, the kids will be the worse for drink...

GLUG GLUG

Zz

...And that she only has a little glass of rum when she's got a cold and that...

Okay! Well, I'm going to try to find room "L."

ROOM L

Ah! It's here!

The magic doll! There it is!

I must open this display case. Gently... gently...

DDRRRAIIIIING !

DRRRRAAAAAiiiiiiiiiNGGGg

The alarm!

Where have they... ₹Hic...₹ put that darn alarm clock?!

Darn it all! There's no way to stop that ringing!

DDRRRAAAiiiiNN

CLAING

GGGDRRAiiii

iNGGDRAAiiiiN

It's at the museum! Quick! Bring out the cars! I'll alert the captain!

BEEP BEEP BEEP

iiiiiiiiNN DRRiiii

The exit? Which way is the exit?

DRRiiiiNNGooo

HALT! WE'VE GOT YOU!

DRRAAii NGD

Why... why, it's a kid!

Yeah! Young people are real sweethearts nowadays. All right. Hands up, or I'll shoot!

GGDRRAAiii

ROOM L

30

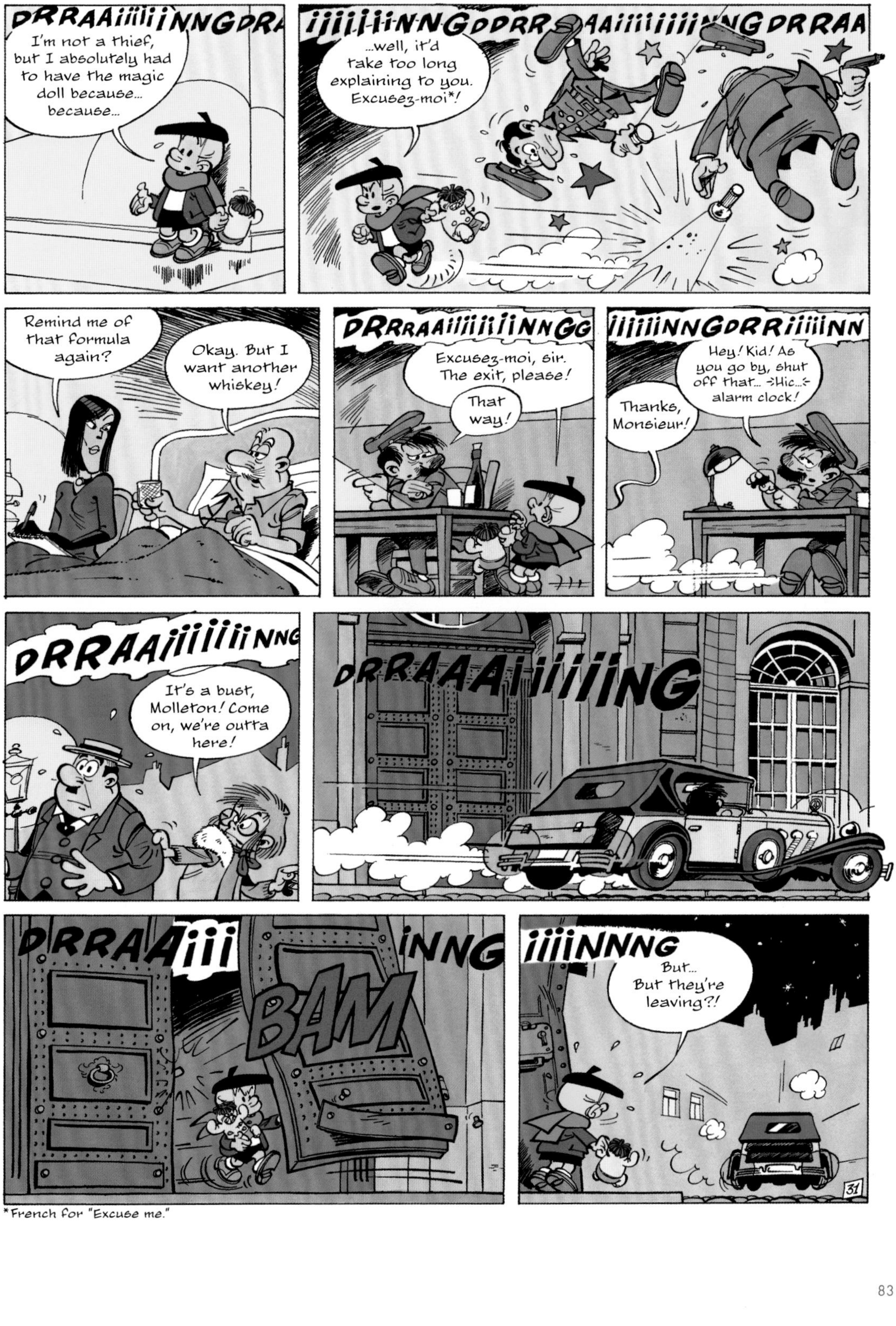
DRRAAiiiiiiINNGDRR
I'm not a thief, but I absolutely had to have the magic doll because... because...
iiiiiiiNNGDDRR AAiiiiiiiiNNGDRRAA
...well, it'd take too long explaining to you. Excusez-moi*!
Remind me of that formula again?
Okay. But I want another whiskey!
DRRRAAiiiiiiiiNNGG
Excusez-moi, sir. The exit, please!
That way!
iiiiiiNNGDRRiiiiiNN
Hey! Kid! As you go by, shut off that... Hic... alarm clock!
Thanks, Monsieur!
DRRAAiiiiiiNNG
It's a bust, Molleton! Come on, we're outta here!
DRRAAAiiiiiiNG
DRRAAiii
INNG
BAM
iiiiNNNG
But... But they're leaving?!
31

*French for "Excuse me."

Hey! Wait! I have it! I have the magic doll!

STOP!

?

Voici*!

Well, my oh my oh my!...

Ah! There are the police.

WAAAAAH

DRRAiiiing

→Whew!←
It's about time!

Madame Demonia will be happy!

Yoohoo! Monsieur Police Captain!

Benny! But what are you doing here?

I'll explain everything to you!

POLICE

DRRAAiiiii

It's very simple! You remember what I told you the other day. Well, I was mistaken because it was to save the Colonel who is her uncle and who's bewitched, that they asked me to because I'm very strong -- but you mustn't tell anyone -- to take the magic doll, but I'm sure that--

Yes, fine, that's all right, I understood. Now, get to bed, it's late, and I have work to do!

But I swear to you that--

There were at least a dozen, Captain!

They've... →Hic...← drugged me with an alarm!

I don't understand! Nothing valuable has disappeared!

32

*French for "Here."

84

The magic doll! The fortune!

And what do we do now, Madame Demonia?

We're off to bed! But starting tomorrow, work! You're going to bring me an object -- a personal one -- from this list of people: the banker, John Delamenouille, Sylvia Samovar the movie star, the jeweler Lepoutre, the cabinet secretary Forty Borre, and Stromboli, the arms dealer.

But... why? What's that...?

That's my business! Go on, it's late! To bed!

The next day...

Hello, Joseph! To the bank!

Yes, Mr. Dela-menouille!

That's him. Let's go!

Don't move. We're armed!

But... what is this? What do you want?

I don't know! Your cigar!

My... my cigar?!

Yeah, your cigar! And quick! All right. We're out of here! Don't move, you two!

?

A hold-up! They organized a hold-up to steal my cigar?!

One down. Now the movie star!

85

NO, Fredini! No, no, and no! I refuse to film in front of that... that scatterbrain who hasn't apologized to me!

Come now, Sylvia...

Calling me an old goat. Me! Sylvia Samovar! Haahaaa!... I'm breaking the contract!

Now, now, Sylvia...

Miss Sylvia Samovar, we're two of your many admirers. Would you be so kind as to give us an autograph?

Yes. Here! On your photo!

We've seen all your movies! You remain the loveliest, most talented, greatest...

Heeheeheehee! Now, now! I'm just an actress like any other!

And there! Who's next?

Me! Me, Sylvia! The unique! The only one! Doing that to me!

Sylvia, darling...

Lepoutre, the diamond dealer!

Maître D'*! My jacket and my hat.

Right away, sir.

I'm sorry, Mister Lepoutre. I don't understand what's happened, but I can't find your hat!

Next. Yikes! The cabinet secretary! That won't be easy. I don't see how we--

Wait! I have an idea! There's a costume shop not far from here! Come!

A file for you, Mr. Secretary.

Set it there.

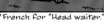
*French for "Head waiter."

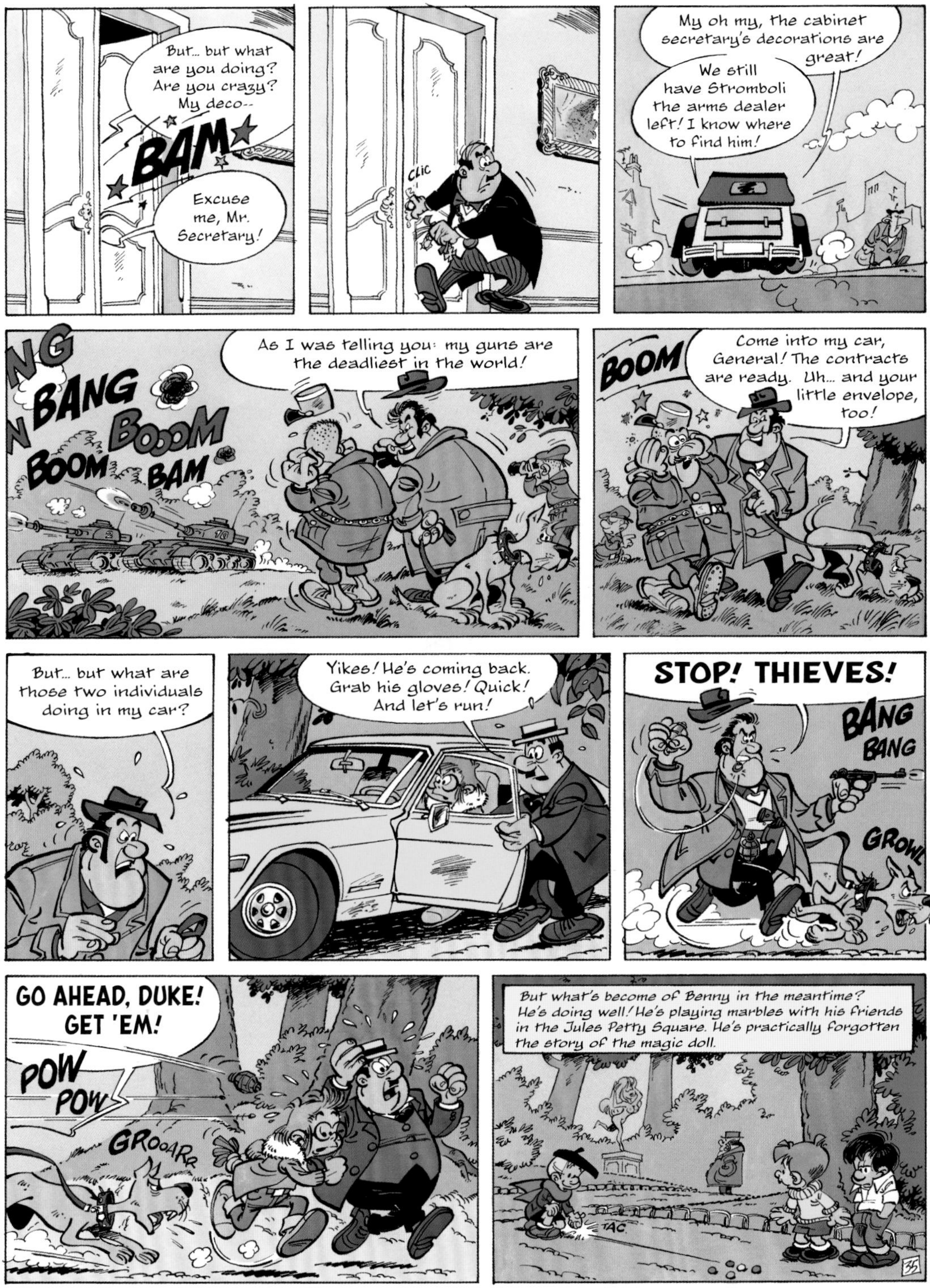
But... but what are you doing? Are you crazy? My deco--
BAM
Excuse me, Mr. Secretary!
CLIC
My oh my, the cabinet secretary's decorations are great!
We still have Stromboli the arms dealer left! I know where to find him!
BANG
BOOOM
BOOM
BAM
As I was telling you: my guns are the deadliest in the world!
BOOM
Come into my car, General! The contracts are ready. Uh... and your little envelope, too!
But... but what are those two individuals doing in my car?
Yikes! He's coming back. Grab his gloves! Quick! And let's run!
STOP! THIEVES!
BANG
BANG
GROWL
GO AHEAD, DUKE! GET 'EM!
POW
POW
GROOARR
But what's become of Benny in the meantime? He's doing well! He's playing marbles with his friends in the Jules Petty Square. He's practically forgotten the story of the magic doll.
TAC

My compliments, Mr. Molleton. Good job, Zlip. You've both done good work!

Yeah. But it was no piece of cake, eh. What a nasty mutt!

And what do we do now?

You're going to change clothes. Don't bother me for any reason!

Okay. I'll start with the movie star.

And then the spell! "WAMBALA BOUBOU..."

CHTAC

And right away!

EEEEEEEE!

!?!

But... but, sir! What's happening to you?

Heavens! It's horrible!

My doctor! Call my doctor and fast!

And there. Now we just have to wait for reactions!

...these five personalities from the world of entertainment, business, and politics...

Called to their bedsides. The most eminent dermatologists are lost in conjectures over this strange illness that...

...their lives don't seem to be in danger, but nothing... CLICK!

Good. Very good. In two or three days, we'll be rich!

36

88

A few days later...

In front of Vivejoie-la-Grande, our troops are holding strong. And the assault, take note, is on the 13th!

Von Paraboum, the colonel of the army

Hey! I wonder if Colonel Bradstone has been cured?

Okay. The fruit must be ripe! Let's go! ...The jeweler...

Hello? Mr. Lepoutre? ...I've heard that you're suffering from a terrible affliction with which I'm well acquainted and have treated before... Yes?...

...and no results? Well, after many years of research, I've found the cure, a cure which only I know!

Why, of course! Unfortunately, it's very expensive and I... Ah!... The price is unimportant? Very well! I'll be at your place in an hour!

There you go. Bring out the car. I'll get the magic doll.

Hey, Benny! Coming to play soccer?

Not today. I'm going to say hello to an old colonel!

Luck can be good or bad sometimes. The fact remains that Benny crosses paths with Madame Demonia's car without realizing it.

Boohoooo! And I was so handsome! Look at me! I'm ugly, repulsive! For pity's sake, do something!

Yes, of course. Calm down! Everything will be okay!

A little sugar, some tomato paste... some... Oh! Whatever!

Now, close your eyes tight and, when I tell you, drink this.

=SNIF!=

Go ahead!

I...I'm cured! **I'M CURED!**

Ah! Madame, how could I ever thank you?

It's simple. Write me my check!

I have a friend, the banker John Delamenouille, who's in the same situation as me and--

Ah, yes?

Meanwhile...

DRINN DRIIIin

Nobody's there! That means the Colonel is cured. I'm really happy for him!

DEMONIA! MY WHISKEY ÷☆!

But that's the Colonel's voice!

BAM

DEMONIA!

What? You're not cured?

What? But... What the... Who are you?

My name is Benny! Madame Demonia and her friends told me you were bewitched, but that the magic doll could save you! So, since I'm very strong, I went to get it at the museum and then I gave it to them.

Ohhhhh! It's not true!

But that magic doll has never cured anyone! On the contrary, it's an evil thing!

"Listen! An old witchdoctor sold it to me during my last trip to Africa."

"On the way back, I was bringing a major collection of pieces of art destined for an international exhibition. The magic doll was in my baggage."

"During the trip, I suddenly came down with a tropical fever!"

CLAC CLAC CLAC

"Upon arrival, I was still very ill. I'm taken away, unconscious. Customs opens my luggage and puts the magic doll in the collection!"

When my fever subsided, I was at a hospital, with a nurse at my bedside. Like an idiot, I told her everything, and right away, she had me brought here. Now that she has the magic doll, she must be using it to do bad stuff!

39

You can't stay here. Get dressed. We're leaving!

Okay. You don't know where the whiskey is?

Hello? Monsieur Dussiflard? Benny, here. I have a favor to ask of you...

And meanwhile, at the banker's home...

No, no. Leave the check to the bearer! Thanks!

I'm the one thanking you!

Everything is fine Now, let's go to the movie star's place!

BEEEP BEEEP?

Ah! There he is!

÷Hic!÷

Monsieur Dussiflard, could you drive this man to Madame Adolphine's and ask her to take care of him?

Why, of course, Benny!

Bye, kid! Be careful! Madame Demonia-- ÷Hic!÷... She's a--

Yes! I know! Goodbye, Colonel!

Okay! Everything's in order in that respect! Now...

÷Hic!÷

...I must find Madame Demonia!

Here! Take my furs, too!... And this jewelry!... Do you want an autograph?

No. The one you wrote on the check is enough for me!

40

Where could they be? The city is big after all!

Okay. I can see only one solution. Jump as high as possible. One... two...

...and hup!

And when Benny says he's going to jump high, it's truly very high!

I don't see them! I'll keep at it!

But where are they?

And from chimneys to gables...

Daddy! I just saw a UFO with a beret and a scarf!

Stop talking nonsense, you son of a fool!

Ah! Zlip and Molleton! There they are!

I know every-thing!

? ?

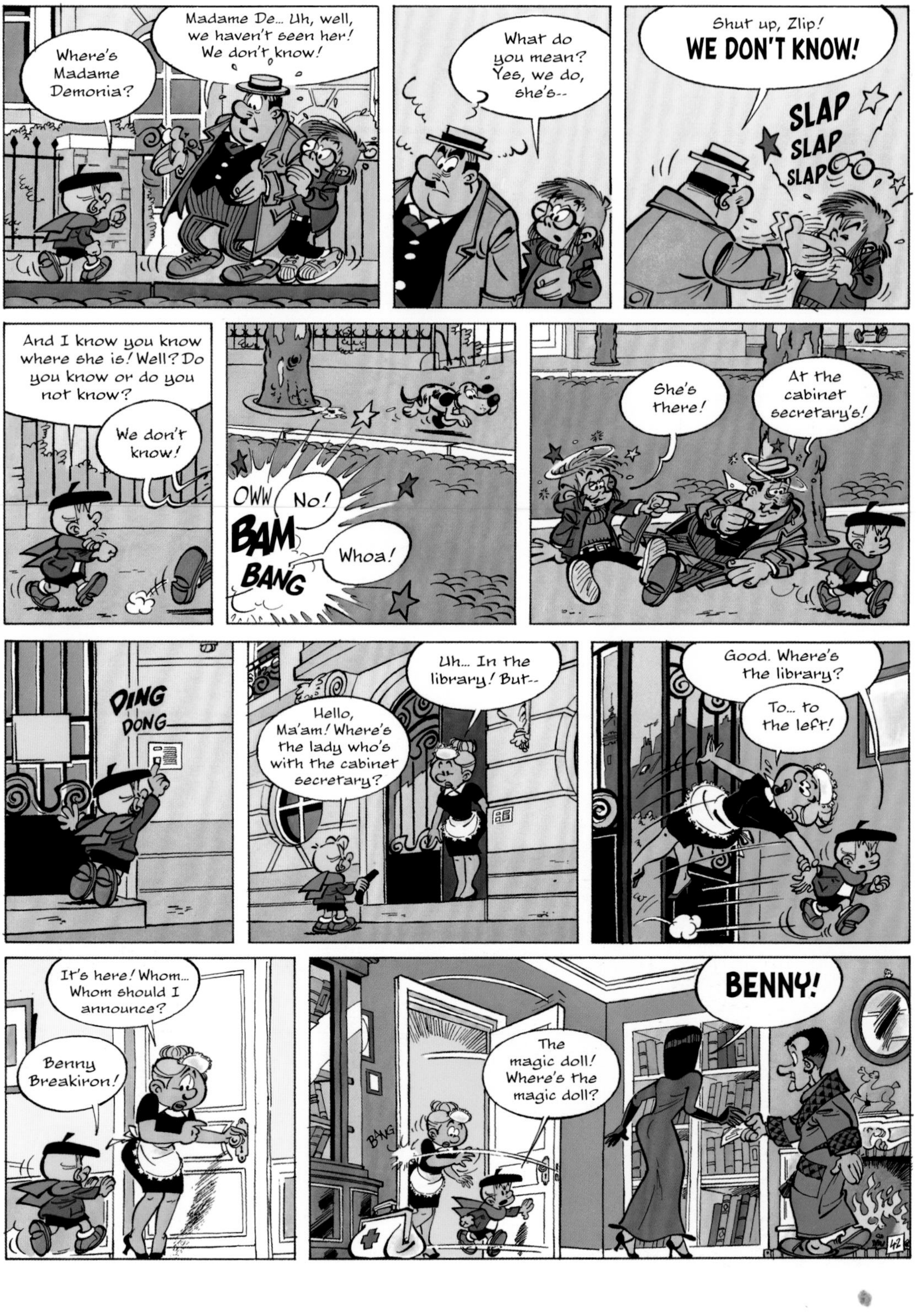

Where's Madame Demonia?
Madame De... Uh, well, we haven't seen her! We don't know!
What do you mean? Yes, we do, she's--
Shut up, Zlip!
WE DON'T KNOW!
SLAP
SLAP
SLAP
And I know you know where she is! Well? Do you know or do you not know?
We don't know!
OWW
No!
BAM
BANG
Whoa!
She's there!
At the cabinet secretary's!
DING
DONG
Uh... In the library! But--
Hello, Ma'am! Where's the lady who's with the cabinet secretary?
Good. Where's the library?
To... to the left!
It's here! Whom... Whom should I announce?
Benny Breakiron!
BENNY!
The magic doll! Where's the magic doll?
BANG

You'll never get it. You'll have to go through me before you'll--

Before nothing at all!

SCRATCH

Give that magic doll back or else...

!

~GRRGL...~

Tell me, dear lady, do you do judo?

No. Why?

Because I'm a black belt!

Excuse me. I think I'd better call the police!

Good job, M.* Secretary!

Hello?

BENNY! NO! WHAT ARE YOU DOING?

I'm burning that dirty magic doll!

NO!

That way it won't hurt anybody else!

SCRITSCRATCH...

43

*M. is short for Monsieur

95

You little wretch! You burned the magic doll, and there was a nail left in! That person can never be disenchanted now!

waaaaaaagaaaAAAAH

THE POLICE!

Here's your coat, Mad-- ?

It's all over! Quick! Let's run!

Shut up, Zlip!

But I didn't say anything!

Ah! There's the police chief!

waaaaaaaaaaaAAH

Benny! Are you here again?

I'm going to tell you everything that's -- Oh! Well, it's no use, you never believe me!

Hey, who, in fact, was the unhappy person whose nail remained in the magic doll and who'll never be cured?... Stromboli, arms dealer!

Oh! That's no big deal!

In the tire? A WHAT?!

A nail, Madame Demonia! A nail!

THE END

SMURFERRIES

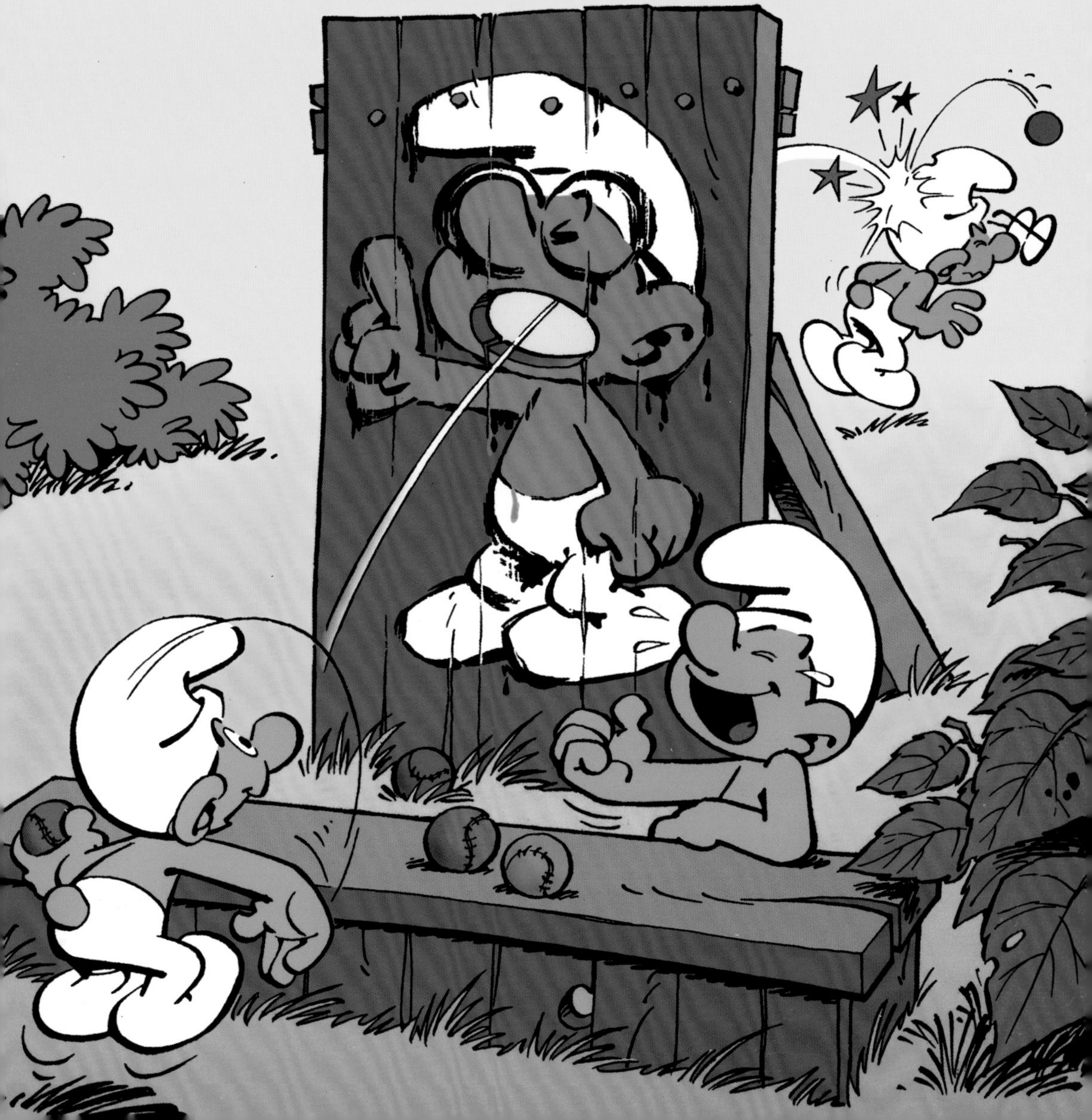

SMURFERRIES

Ah! I think I've finally smurfed that shrinking potion!

I've been smurfing on the formula for more than ten years.

Oops! What a klutz!

Luckily there's a drop left!

SLURP

Smurf! Well, once again, it didn't work!

I'm giving up! I'll NEVER smurf it!

NEVER! NEVER! Never!

So has Baby Smurf picked which musical instrument he's going to play?

Sadly not! It's a disaster!

We've tried everything, but he doesn't seem to like any of them! You'll see...

TULULULUUUUU

WAAAAAH!

DOODOOMBEDOOM

WAAAAAH!

TINGALINGATING DING

WAAH!

CLANG BOOM
DOOBOOBOODOOM

WAAAH!

PWAAAT

Wait! I know an instrument he's sure to like!

?

OOAAAOOAAAAOOAAAAOOOAAA

Arhoo!

! ?

8

Ah! It's so nice living in our little village! Every Smurf has their place and can smurf their own talents...

...Like Lumberjack Smurf. There he is smurfing a tree...

Hefty Smurf smurfs the trunks to the Carpenter Smurf's sawmill...

...Who smurfs them into different size boards...

Handy Smurf smurfs the boards to smurf different kinds of furniture... Like Smurfette's new bed...

BAM BAM

Tailor Smurf smurfs the smurfiest fabric for the sheets, while the other little Smurfs gather down for the comforter...

RRRRZZZZz RRRrrr

Hmm! But, there's one Smurf in the village who doesn't smurf!

RRRRrrr ZZZZZz!

Oh, yes! Even Lazy Smurf is smurfing his share of the work: he's testing the bed!

67

...Hefty Smurf will smurf the wood. Handy Smurf will fix the well. And Lazy Smurf will sweep the village square...

PFFF!

Sweeper! That's smurfing work!

What smurfousness! I'm fed up with smurfing the smurf like a smurf!

What do I hear? I'd like you to smurf your work without smurfing smurferries!

Good! Keep working like that!

SCRAT SCRAT SCRAT

?

Now we're talking!

© Peyo

71

Wait, that's right! Today's the impersonation party. Every Smurf has to smurf another Smurf...

Handy Smurf is smurfing Baker Smurf... Hmm!

Hey there, y'all smurfs! Well, howdy, Papa Smurf!

Hee! Hee! Hee! Smurfette's acting like Farmer Smurf!

Here! I have a cake for you!

Oh?

?

Ho! Ho! Bravo, Baker Smurf! Great imitation of Jokey Smurf!

PROUTCH

Poet Smurf smurfs everyone instead of Brainy Smurf. And Brainy Smurf's trying to imitate Hefty Smurf! Chin up!

So Greedy Smurf's smurfing into the shoes of Lazy Smurf?

Oh, no, Papa Smurf... I'm huuuungry! He who sleeps, eats, my smurf!

GROWL GRMBL

How about you, Jokey Smurf? Who did you decide to imitate?

Not now, my little Smurf! I have to smurf an important experiment in my laboratory...

Now, then! Who does he think he's smurfing?!

© Peyo - 63 -

103

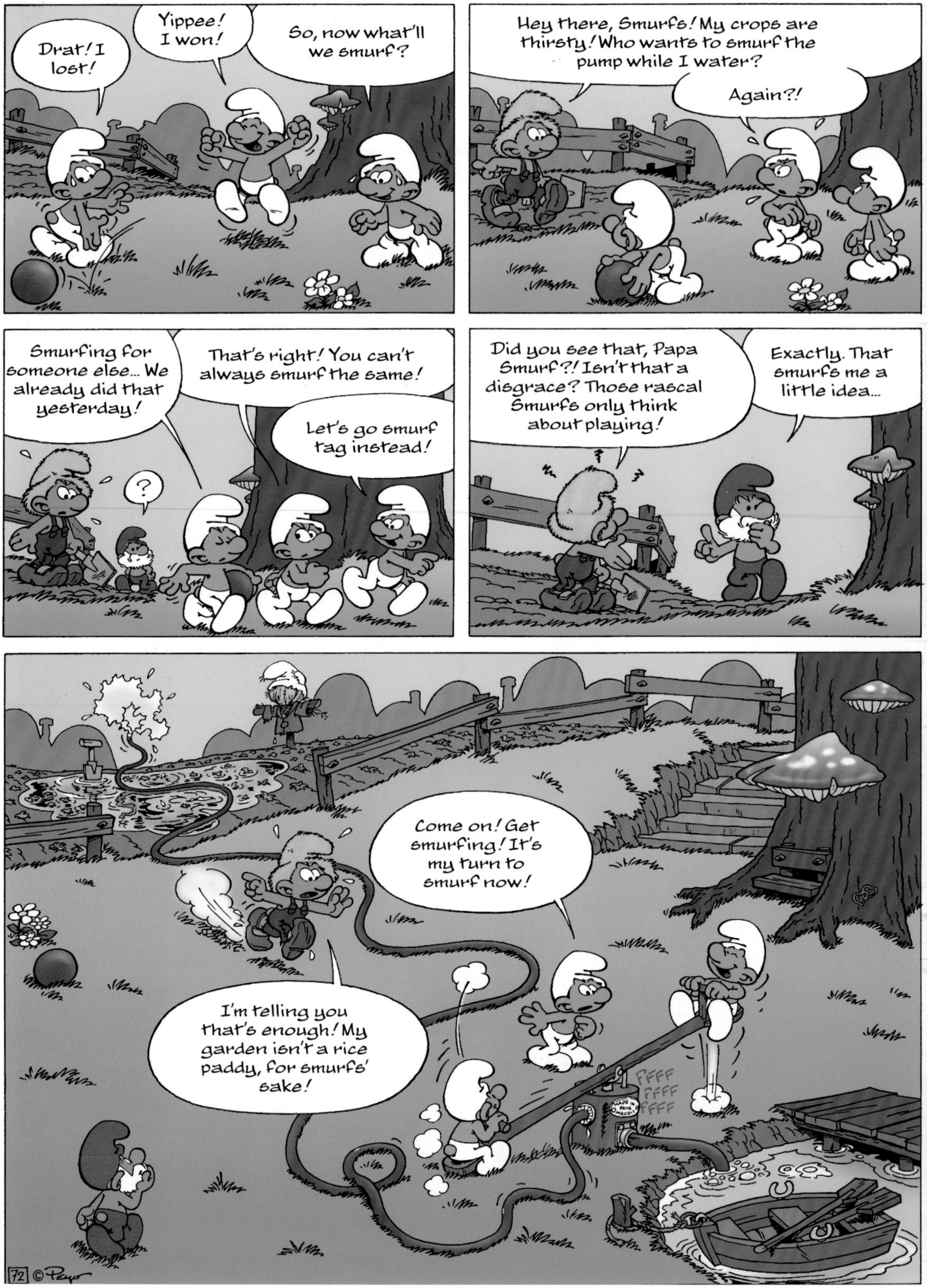
Drat! I lost!
Yippee! I won!
So, now what'll we smurf?
Hey there, Smurfs! My crops are thirsty! Who wants to smurf the pump while I water?
Again?!
Smurfing for someone else... We already did that yesterday!
That's right! You can't always smurf the same!
Let's go smurf tag instead!
?
Did you see that, Papa Smurf?! Isn't that a disgrace? Those rascal Smurfs only think about playing!
Exactly. That smurfs me a little idea...
Come on! Get smurfing! It's my turn to smurf now!
I'm telling you that's enough! My garden isn't a rice paddy, for smurfs' sake!
FFFF FFFF FFFF
72 © Peyo

RAM BLAM RATAPLAN

AN ANNOUNCEMENT FOR ALL SMURFS!

..... ? Well? Smurf your announcement! We're listening! ?

I... I suddenly can't smurf! It's awful! This has never smurfed to me before!

Come, come! Don't smurf in a tizzy! Take your time! That'll resmurf you!

A little later...

A lot later.

Ah, it came back!

ALL SMURFS SHOULD GO TO THE DAM TO SMURF EMERGENCY REPAIRS!

?

© Peyo 74

Heavens, I've smurfed another 3 grams!

I'm going to have to go on a diet...

Hey, Smurfette! I'm going to smurf you a nice cake like you smurf!

Oh, no! Absolutely not! I'm on a diet!

Or else, with only a teeny tiny bit of flour!

Some almonds... Not too much sugar... A tiny little banana... A hint of chocolate...

A touch of cream... A pat of butter...

There! It's smurfed! But I don't know about your waistline...

Mmm! It's perfect! I've never smurfed such a good diet cake!

5

AZRAEL!

Where've you been just now?

MEOW!

If you could just imagine the danger the heroes smurf in this story, Baby Smurf!

Peyo

Smurf! Baker Smurf forgot to smurf me how much yeast is used to smurf this cake.

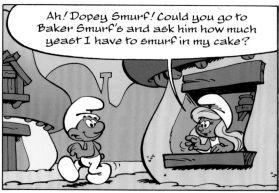

Ah! Dopey Smurf! Could you go to Baker Smurf's and ask him how much yeast I have to smurf in my cake?

Dopey Smurf?...Hmm! He's sure to smurf up the amount!

HEY! DOPEY SMURF! WAIT!

Ask him to smurf the exact number on a piece of paper!

I forgot to smurf how much yeast? Oh, my, my! That's me all over!

Let's see... Ah! Here! Yeast: 186 grams exactly!

I have to smurf it in writing: one hundred eighty-six...

Here, Smurfette! Nine hundred eighty-one. Thanks, Dopey Smurf!

DOPEY SMURF!

55

Heh! Heh! I'm on the right smurf! I'm sure I'll discover it!...

And Baker Smurf will reward me by smurfing me a big cake!...

Well, hello! What're you smurfing?

I'm smurfing a trail... Do you see all these crumbs?

A-a trail? Of crumbs? Uh... Yessss, so what?

Shh! ...Not so loud... He mustn't be far... A thief smurfed a cake from Baker Smurf's again...

Oh?... Uh... And you smurfed some clues?

A lot! He went into Baker Smurf's through the garden door... And there're only mud and brambles in the garden... Plus a big cake like the one that was smurfed should smurf some traces, right?

Okay, I'll smurf you! I don't want to lose my track so close to the goal!

That's right! Good smurfing, Dopey Smurf!

54

109

It's nice of you to give me a scarf, Dopey Smurf, but should I smurf it in this heat?

Hee! Hee! Hee! Sunglasses! I don't know when I'll be able to wear them but thanks, Dopey Smurf. Hee! Hee! Hee!

Thanks for the present, Dopey Smurf, but really, no thanks!

Well now, Dopey Smurf! You don't seem like you're smurfing!

No, Jokey Smurf. I do everything wrong...

Every time I smurf a Smurf a present, they smurf at my smurf, because they can't use my present.

Of course, Dopey Smurf! You have to pick your present by smurfing the Smurf you want to give it to. Do you understand?

Oh?! Then I think you should like this present.

A present? For me?

PROUF

So, did you like it?

65

Heh, heh, heh!...

There's Baker Smurf with a present like mine!

I'd better smurf the other Smurfs!

It's mine to smurf!

I'll smurf his and leave mine!

Yum! What a nice cake!

?

NOC
NOC
NOC

Happy birthday, Jokey Smurf! We've brought you this lovely cake!

38

:Pfff...: What a smurfery!

What's wrong, Chef Smurf?

I'm exhausted, Handy Smurf! Parties are great, but there's no smurfing washing the dishes the day after!

Hmm... Maybe I could smurf something for you...

I think I've got an idea... Leave all that! I'll come back tomorrow with a solution to your problem...

Great! Thanks, Handy Smurf!

The next day...

There, Chef Smurf! Smurf on the bike while I smurf the dirty dishes into the machine...

?

Done! You can start smurfing for it to wash...

BA BANG CLANK

Next, the rinse cycle! Faster! Faster!

ROLL ROLL ROLL ROLL

And now I'll smurf the fan for the drying cycle! A little bit more, Chef Smurf!

RRRRR RRRRR

Hee! Hee! The dishes are all clean! So what do you think, Chef Smurf?

Isn't it less tiring smurfing the dishes this way...?

Chef Smurf?

69

OOOAAH! Such lovely sunshine! The day looks to be smurfy!

Come on! I shouldn't dawdle!

Today, Papa Smurf said we'd smurf at the dam...

I really like smurfing at the dam!

This weather is perfect for smurfing!

Ah! This spot seems good to me!

Nobody's seen Lazy Smurf?

113

Hello! What beautiful smurf for the season, don't you think?

That's right! I'm taking the opportunity to smurf my leeks!

I'm going to smurf the day in the meadow and work on my ode, "Buttercups, Cornflowers, and Smurfpoppies!"

Why smurf so far?

You could stay here and smurf a poem about my leeks, carrots, and cabbages!

WHAT?

A poem about vegetables, what an idea! Farmer Smurf, you make me laugh!

Cornflowers lose their power
Smurfpoppies smurf all floppy.

Buttercups sleep standing up;
They're no longer stronger
When twilight smurfs flight...

There, that's a smurfly nice one!

Enough smurfing for today. It's time to return, I'd say!

Hmm! Farmer Smurf's house smells smurfly good!

Say! Will you smurf me a nice bowl of your delicious cabbage soup?

No, but I smurfed a pot just for you...

...of buttercups, cornflowers, and smurfpoppies!

43

Peyo

114

I smurfed some very nice verses this afternoon. The countryside always smurfs me inspiration!

You smurf them in comfort! I have to fight plants that invade my fields and it's a fine smurfery!

POC

Farmer Smurf, you can't appreciate beautiful things! Look...

Poppies, cornflowers, and buttercups... Hasn't nature smurfed all that to make our walks a delight?

Really? Then smurf over here!

There! Brambles, nettles, and thistles. Who do you think would be smurf enough to walk through them?

© Peyo

Hey, Grouchy Smurf! Where're you smurfing? The smurfworks are about to start!

Me, I don't like smurfworks!

Me, I don't like flares, I don't like explosions, I don't like smoke...

PFFF! Too bad for you!

Oh! A pretty blue one!

Oh! A pretty red one!

Me, I don't like blue ones! And me, I don't like red ones!

And there! A pretty green one!

Oh! Look out! It didn't smurf!

?

Well done! I really like rockets that don't smurf!

?

BANG

OOOH! A PRETTY BLACK ONE!

Me, I don't like ANY smurfworks!

© Peyo

73

But... But Clumsy Smurf! Stop! What're you smurfing again?

Look! You're smurfing on the wrong side of the branch again!

If you continue, you're going to smurf your face! You need to smurf on the other side!

Like this?

Yes! Like that!

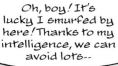

Oh, boy! It's lucky I smurfed by here! Thanks to my intelligence, we can avoid lots--

BOp

--of stupid accidents!

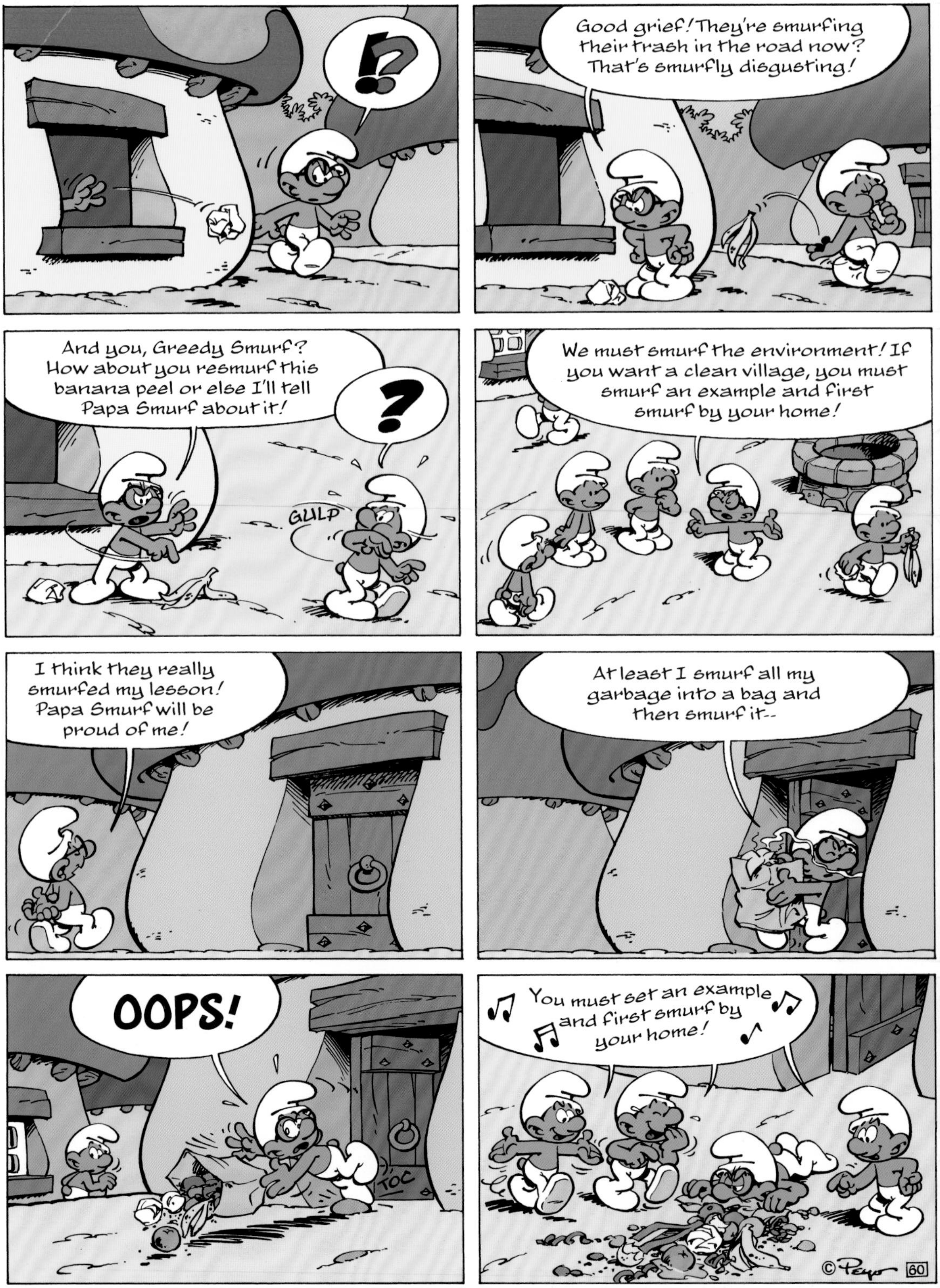
!?
Good grief! They're smurfing their trash in the road now? That's smurfly disgusting!
And you, Greedy Smurf? How about you resmurf this banana peel or else I'll tell Papa Smurf about it!
?
GULP
We must smurf the environment! If you want a clean village, you must smurf an example and first smurf by your home!
I think they really smurfed my lesson! Papa Smurf will be proud of me!
At least I smurf all my garbage into a bag and then smurf it--
OOPS!
TOC
You must set an example and first smurf by your home!
© Peyo
60

Believe me, Jokey Smurf! I'm not Alchemist Smurf for nothing! We're really going to smurf!

Yes! Hee! Hee! Hee! I really smurf it! Hmm! Careful! There he is!

Hello, Brainy Smurf! Since you're our leader while Papa Smurf's away, we wanted to smurf you this.

Ah, what is it?

It's a magic potion that will smurf you the most IMPRESSIVE Smurf in the village!

The most impressive? Oh, thank you, Jokey Smurf! I'll use it for my speech this evening!

That evening.

Dear Smurfs and Smurfette--

Oops, I almost forgot my potion...

We're going to laugh!

...which should make me the Smurf who's the most--

POOF

--IMPRESSIVE

?!

HA! HA! HA!

RIIIP

Jokey Smurf! Come here!... I'm going to tell Papa Smurf!

Tailor Smurf, there's some work here for you!

© Peyo 68

Say, Brainy Smurf! Could you look after this frog for me?... Just long enough for me to smurf a favor for Papa Smurf!

Your frog?!... But... uh... certainly!

A frog, that's fun!...That's the sign that the smurf of nice weather's here!

Hey?!... It's climbing out! The weather's going to be nice!

Let's enjoy it! I'm going to smurf by the river!

Ah, well, no! It's smurfing all the way at the bottom! Then that means it'll be cold and damp!

Okay! If that's what it says!

Hey! I have to tell you that your frog is a bit off with its forecasts!

Oh? But that isn't MY frog...

...It's Dopey Smurf's!

© Peyo 57

I'm going to hang this pretty portrait that Painter Smurf smurfed of me!

OW!

PAF

?

Quick, Smurfs! Vanity Smurf hurt himself badly!

OWIEOWIE OUCHIEOUCHIE! OUCH!

Don't move! We'll take care of you!

Help me smurf him into his room!

I'll go find Smurfette!

There! That's for the big boo-boo!

Poor Vanity Smurf! He looks so cozy!

Let him rest now...

In fact, he's already smurfing!

ZZZ

I'm going to hang his picture!

OW!

PAF

≥SHHHHH!≤ Come on, not so loud! You'll wake him up!

52

He smurfs well, eh?

Yes! He's smurfly got talent.

But--But he's smurfing on the wall of my smurf?!

NO! IT'S NOT OKAY THERE, SMURF! I'll smurf you an hour to repaint all of that!

Such a shame! It's pretty, though!

Yes, great artists are always misunderstood!

And remember... I don't want to smurf a single one of your little pictures!

Anyway, he isn't a bad Smurf!

Since he doesn't want any more of my little pictures!...

Ah! I see he understood that he's met his match with a Smurf like me!

There! MAGNIFICENT! I'm smurfly proud of myself!

Hello, Painter Smurf! Did you smurf a new painting?

Well, yes! What do you smurf of it?

Hefty Smurf will be happy to see his portrait! It's smurf!

?

But... That isn't Hefty Smurf! You don't recognize the Smurf I smurfed?

Well...

Oh! Dopey Smurf! Hey, you didn't smurf it!

It isn't Dopey Smurf?

OF COURSE NOT!

Hello? You painted a portrait of Lazy Smurf?

Anyway, that isn't Dopey Smurf!

Maybe it's Jokey Smurf—

THAT'S ENOUGH! EVERYONE OUT!

...or Grouchy Smurf?

Fine! Since nobody recognizes which smurf I smurfed...

You painted my portrait, Painter Smurf? Thanks! It looks just like me!

Oh, it wasn't hard!

28

Peyo

123

? (speech bubble with alien text)

What's that smurf?

?!

(alien text speech bubble)

I don't understand anything he's smurfing!

(alien text speech bubble)

Did you see how strange he is, with that long smurf?

Hmmm... I understand what he's smurfing perfectly well... He says he smurfs from another planet and that he's thirsty!

Δ !

Δη Δ∇ε̂ϲ !
BLUB !

Bʟ Glug glug... Stop! ...glug... It's me, Jokey Smurf!

And now? What's he smurfing?

Ah! You're thirsty?... Come on! I'll smurf you a little water!

(alien text speech bubble)

© Peyo

56

124

NO!...Smurf! That isn't it!

What're you smurfing, Brainy Smurf?

Crossword puzzles! But they aren't easy!

I can help you if you'd like.

HA!HA!HA! You, Dopey Smurf? Why not, after all?

Let's see. "Making music," in eight letters... The first letter is an "S"?...

"Smurfing"!

"Smurfing"? HA!HA!HA! Darn Dopey, Smurf! That would be a little too easy! Huh?!... But, yes! That works!

Of course!

Harder now... "Smurfing" in four letters. The third letter is a "K"--

"Make!"

That's right! In five letters, "small shrub"?

"Smurf."

Okay! "Smurf baba" in four letters!

"Cake..."

In three letters...

A little bit later...

Bravo, Dopey Smurf! I can't get over it! You smurfed the whole puzzle!

I promise you, Papa Smurf! It's incredible! He smurfed all the right answers! DOPEY SMURF! Do you realize?!

Anyway, crossword puzzles are really dumb! All you have to do is smurf the answers right above them on the other side!

©Peyo 62

125

Ahaa! You lose! Next!

TAC

¡POC

Heh! Heh! Heh! So who wants to smurf their chance now?

How conceited! Hefty Smurf is nauseating!

Yeah! Too bad none of us could smurf him!

Hey, you go, Dopey Smurf! You haven't tried yet!

?

Look out, Dopey Smurf, here goes!

TAK POC
TOC POC
TAK

Yikes! Tough opponent!

TAC

TAC TAC
TAC TAC
TAC TAC

Oh, my smurfness! That's it, Dopey Smurf! I admit defeat!

HURRAH! LONG LIVE DOPEY SMURF!

Give me five, Dopey Smurf! But how did you smurf the ball so quickly?

?

The ball? What ball! I was just trying to smurf that wasp that's smurfing around! Help! Help me!

© Peyo

64

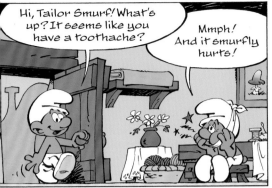

Hi, Tailor Smurf! What's up? It seems like you have a toothache?

Mmph! And it smurfly hurts!

Wait! I know an extreme method for smurfing it! Look! I smurf the end of a string around your tooth...

Mmph?

...And I smurf the other end to that door, which I'll slam really hard!

...You're shure thath...

Don't worry! You've got nothing to smurf! Look out! Here goes!

SLAM

OUCH!

BANG

PAF

POW

Tailor Smurf?!

Well, okay! But at least smurf that thanks to me you don't have a toothache anymore!

58

© Peyo

127

Oh! It smurfed last night!

YIPPEE! I love snow! I don't know anything more smurfing!

We can go skiing! That's smurf! I really want to try!

...Or smurf a smurfman! That's fun, too!

Okay, then! Skiing or smurfman?

Smurfman or skiing?

Skiing is smurf! After all, it's still more smurfing than a--

OOPS!

--than a smurfman!

Smurf over, you're going to see a show!

¿Tsss...¿ He's such a braggart!

!

HA! HA! HA!

Well done, so there!

These skates aren't sharp enough! No way to smurf with equipment like this!

HA! HA! HA!

Don't you think they're smurfed enough like this?

No, no! Keep going! They have to smurf the ice well!

Ah! These skates are well smurfed!

Still so conceited!

Smurf this! I'm going to smurf a perfect circle!

Ah! That's clever!

So where will we smurf now?!

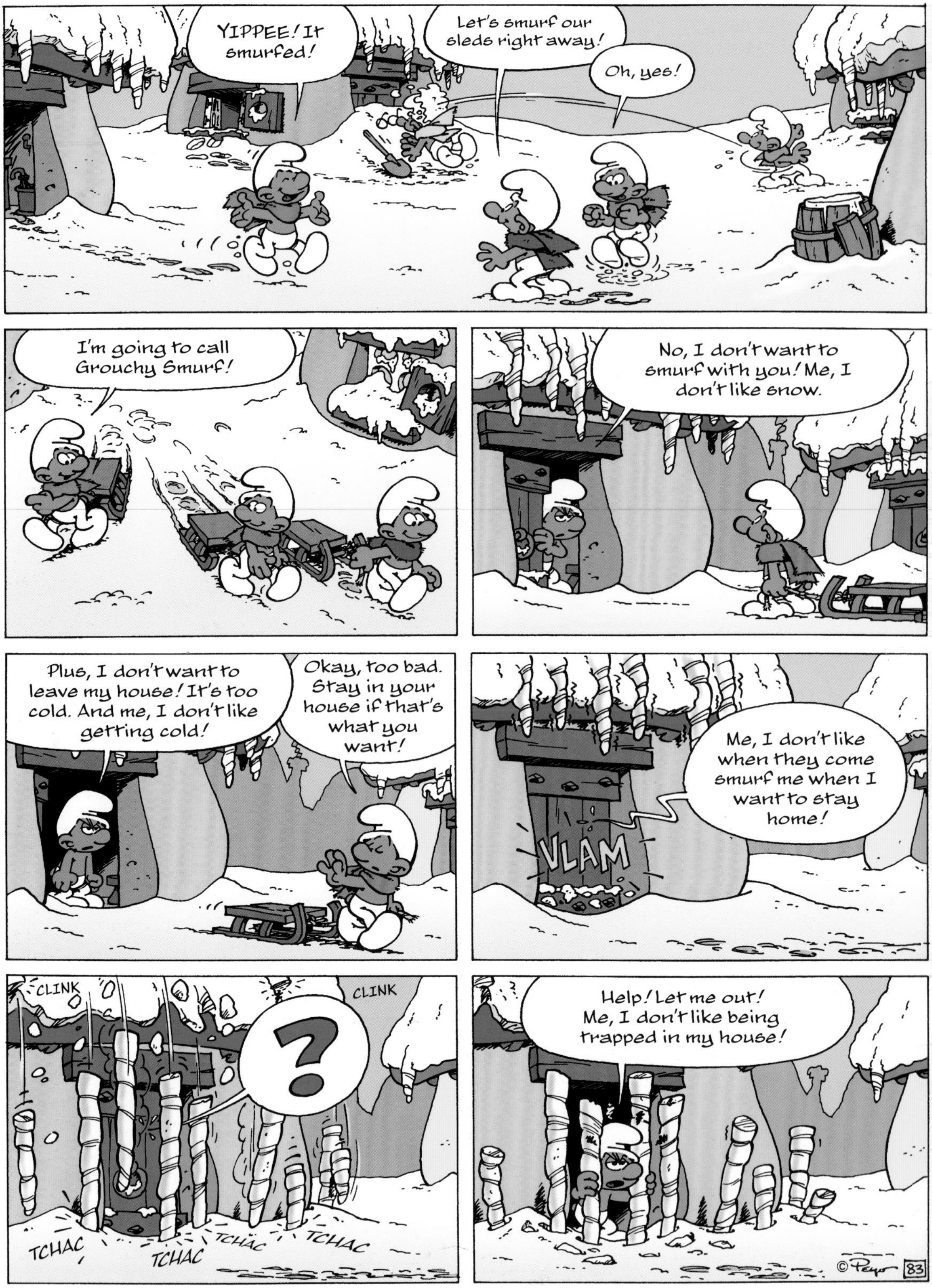

YIPPEE! It smurfed!
Let's smurf our sleds right away!
Oh, yes!
I'm going to call Grouchy Smurf!
No, I don't want to smurf with you! Me, I don't like snow.
Plus, I don't want to leave my house! It's too cold. And me, I don't like getting cold!
Okay, too bad. Stay in your house if that's what you want!
VLAM
Me, I don't like when they come smurf me when I want to stay home!
CLINK
CLINK
?
TCHAC
TCHAC
TCHAC
TCHAC
Help! Let me out! Me, I don't like being trapped in my house!
© Peyo 83

Handy Smurf, could you lend me a smurf wrench?

Uh... Yes, Papa Smurf...

But it'll take me a minute to smurf my hands on it!

I'll ask someone else. But frankly, Handy Smurf, you should be ashamed of smurfing in such a mess!

Papa Smurf's right! I need to clean up a bit!

A little later...

Papa Smurf, come look!

It's amazing! I'm smurfed!

Bravo, Handy Smurf! You smurfed an outstanding job!

Papa Smurf was really happy! That makes me glad!

BANG
CLANG
CLONG
TOC

© Peyo 77

Where are you? I'm going to smurf you!

Hee! Hee! Hee! This way!

Ah! I've smurfed one! You... you're... Oh!

Hmm!

My little Smurfs, I know you really like to play, but you could perhaps smurf something useful for once...

Uh... Like what, Papa Smurf?

For example, smurfing a little bit of paint on the roof of the laboratory, which really needs it...

≥PFFF!≤

You'll see. Working can also be very smurfing!

Later...

Look out! There he is!

?

There! That should smurf them a world of good! I'll come back soon to see how they're smurfing...

78

So, Hefty Smurf, how's the swimming workout smurfing?

Mmmyeah, Papa Smurf, mostly good...

Except for Lazy Smurf, who slipped away to smurf a siesta on the little island...

LAZY SMURF! I said "swimming," not "napping"?

Huh? What?!

⸘Pfff!⸰ I can never smurf in peace!

He dove in but I smurfed sight of him...

He must be smurfing underwater...

He's smurfing a long time without coming back up!

Yes! He smurfs very well when he wants to!

You can't smurf that long underwater! He must have smurfed an accident!

Quick!

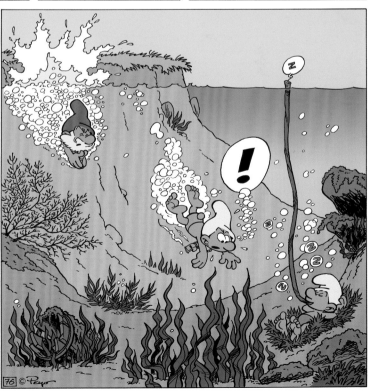

z

!

z

76 © Peyo

133

I've got an idea! What if we smurf them with colors?

?

Hee! Hee! That smurfs! We're going to smurf the greens and the reds.

OH! MY LAUNDRY!

Hee! Hee! Hee! We're sure having a blast!

Hey, you two! I know another way to have fun with water and soap!

You and your smurfy ideas!

85

You're going to smurf water from the well? Smurf careful with the stone on the rim that's loose...

Yes, yes...

SPLOOSH

!

BRAINY SMURF?

It's awful! Brainy Smurf fell into the well! I see his hat there!

We have to smurf him out of there! Smurf me into the well!

Okay, Hefty Smurf!

That's the third time he's gone down...

There he is... Still alone! Bring him back up!

I don't understand it... I should've smurfed him!

¿Sniff!¿ We... We have to let Papa Smurf know!

What's smurf-- OH!! Hefty Smurf! You fell into the well?! That almost happened to me just now...

⁈⁉

Luckily, I was paying attention and only my hat smurfed into the well! I ran home to smurf another one... As for you, Hefty Smurf, you should've been more careful! For that matter, Papa Smurf always says that--

I'M TELLING PAPA SMURF!

© Peyo 79

135

Ho! Ho! I have a feeling it's really going to smurf!

Be a sport, Dopey Smurf! Go smurf some leeks quickly while I pack things up!

Yes, Farmer Smurf!

Here are your leeks, Farmer Smurf!

?!

NO, NO, DOPEY SMURF! THOSE THERE ARE ONIONS!

Oh, yeah?

Darn Dopey Smurf! Sometimes I wonder what goes on in his head?

Well, now! It's starting to smurf!

Dopey Smurf! You're going to get soaked! Do like me! Smurf a leaf of sarsparilla!

Oh, yeah?

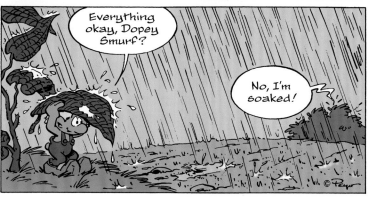

Everything okay, Dopey Smurf?

No, I'm soaked!

The sarsparilla's good, ⸮crunch,⸮ but it doesn't help with the rain much... ⸮Gulp!⸮

80

136

But they aren't smurfing from the tree yet... Pity!

That can be arranged!

Oh! A chestnut tree!

Hmmm... Chestnuts are smurfly good!

HOH!

TOC

BONK

!

Missed! This time I'm going to smurf it on the mark!

TOC

SMURF! Missed again! It's smurfly hard!

BONK

Hey, you two! You could try too, instead of smurfing a siesta!

© Peyo

81

Ah! Here are some smurfly nice ones!

This one will smurf the job perfectly.

Yes, it's smurf!

The weather's really smurf for the season!

It's true! The sun's smurfing brightly!

Here... This will be perfect!

Ah! It's time to smurf our food!

Woowww! I smurfed pepper and salt!

YUM!

It's smurfly good when it's well done!

© Peyo

75

I'm going to smurf you a little tune on my new instrument!

TSWAAA SWAAA!

Okay, I'm going to smurf supper!

I need to smurf my exercises!

I'm going to smurf my field!

TSWAA SWAA SWAA

TSWAAA TSWAA TSWA

It's really smurf of you to stay till the end, Blacksmith Smurf! I'm glad you smurf my music!

Well...

I think it's really interesting! Can you smurf a long time like that?

Me? I could smurf all day long without getting tired!

WONDERFUL! Follow me!

Very good! Above all, smurf in rhythm!

BING BING BING

TSWAAAPWEEEEET TSWAAAPWEEEEET TSWAAAPWEEEEET

86

139

It's nice of you to help me, Clumsy Smurf, but--

Oh, drat!

CRASH

But still, Clumsy Smurf, pay a bit of attention! That's the fifth plate you've smurfed!

?

Come on, Chef Smurf, don't be so harsh! And you, Clumsy Smurf, pay more attention and everything will smurf well!

CLINK
GLINK
GLINK

Did you see? I didn't smurf a single one!

YIPPEE!

© Peyo

88

This raspberry brandy cake is a thing of beauty! They're going to smurf their lips!

HEY, YOU!

GREEDY SMURF! ⊙※☆‼ Thief! Have you no shame?

That Greedy Smurf! He's going to regret it...

NOC NOC

?

Chef Smurf!

What? You dare resmurf here? Go away, Greedy Smurf!

Just a question... Where did you smurf the brandy for your cake?

Uh, well, from Papa Smurf's laboratory, as usual!

I think you smurfed the wrong vial!

Oh, come on, why do you smurf that?

Since I ate that cake, I've felt all smurf!

!?

© Peyo

82

141

But... what's he smurfing?

What the smurf, all of a sudden! I can't even see the tip of my smurf!

Maybe it's one of Gargamel's dirty smurfs! Careful...

Uh... Is that you, Papa Smurf?!

Don't worry, my little smurfs. This thick fog is just from a failed experiment... There's no smurf to fear... Anyway... I hope not...

What was the experiment?

Um! A product to smurf fire without any smoke... It's not at all ready yet...

Ah! It looks like it's starting to clear!

When it smurfs a little bit brighter, make sure there aren't any changes or weird smurfs, still... You never know!

Papa Smurf? It's Chef Smurf here! I think I smurfed something weird...

Oh? Show me, Chef Smurf!

I put my cakes on the windowsill to cool and they've disappeared! Do you think your fog smurfed them?

Hmm! My fog has something to do with it because I think someone smurfed away in it... Right, Greedy Smurf?

Today, like every market day, the people of the town of Aubenas are peacefully going about their business...

Unbeknownst to them, however...

Careful! Let's be discreet...

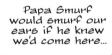

Papa Smurf would smurf our ears if he knew we'd come here...

Okay, we'll have to smurf to that fence without getting spotted!

Over there? No way!

I knew you were nothing but fraidysmurfs! Ready...?

SMURF FOR IT!

SCRITCH

Hey, wait! Your sack got smurfed on a nail!

© Peyo [1]

143

Good try! Last one there's a smurf!

Ha! Ha! Ha! I'm always first when Hefty Smurf's not around!

⇒CHOKE!⇐ ⇒KOF!⇐ ⇒KOF! KOF!⇐

?

Oooo... I'm sure Chef Smurf won't want to smurf me an extra dessert now!

ATCHOO!

Can you smurf me a little from your sack?

No way! Otherwise I'm the one risking not smurfing a dessert!

KOF KOF

AHA! KNAVE! YOUR FINAL HOUR HAS COME!

?

!?

?

You have no chance!

CLANG

!

© Peyo

You see that? It's a tournament!

GO, RED PLUME!

?

GO AHEAD, KNOCK THEM DOWN!

Excuse me, milord, it seems to me your favorite is in trouble!

!

Bailiff, you're naught but a fool! I'll bet you two crowns he'll crush his opponent!

Deal, milord!

I bet my smock on the red one!

Deal! The blue one's going to smash him!

?

It's true the blue one looks smurfly stronger than the red one!

÷Hmmpf!÷

CLING

Red hasn't smurfed his last say!

3

Blue's going to win! Smurf him to pieces!

Don't let yourself be smurfed, Red!

?

© Peyo

145

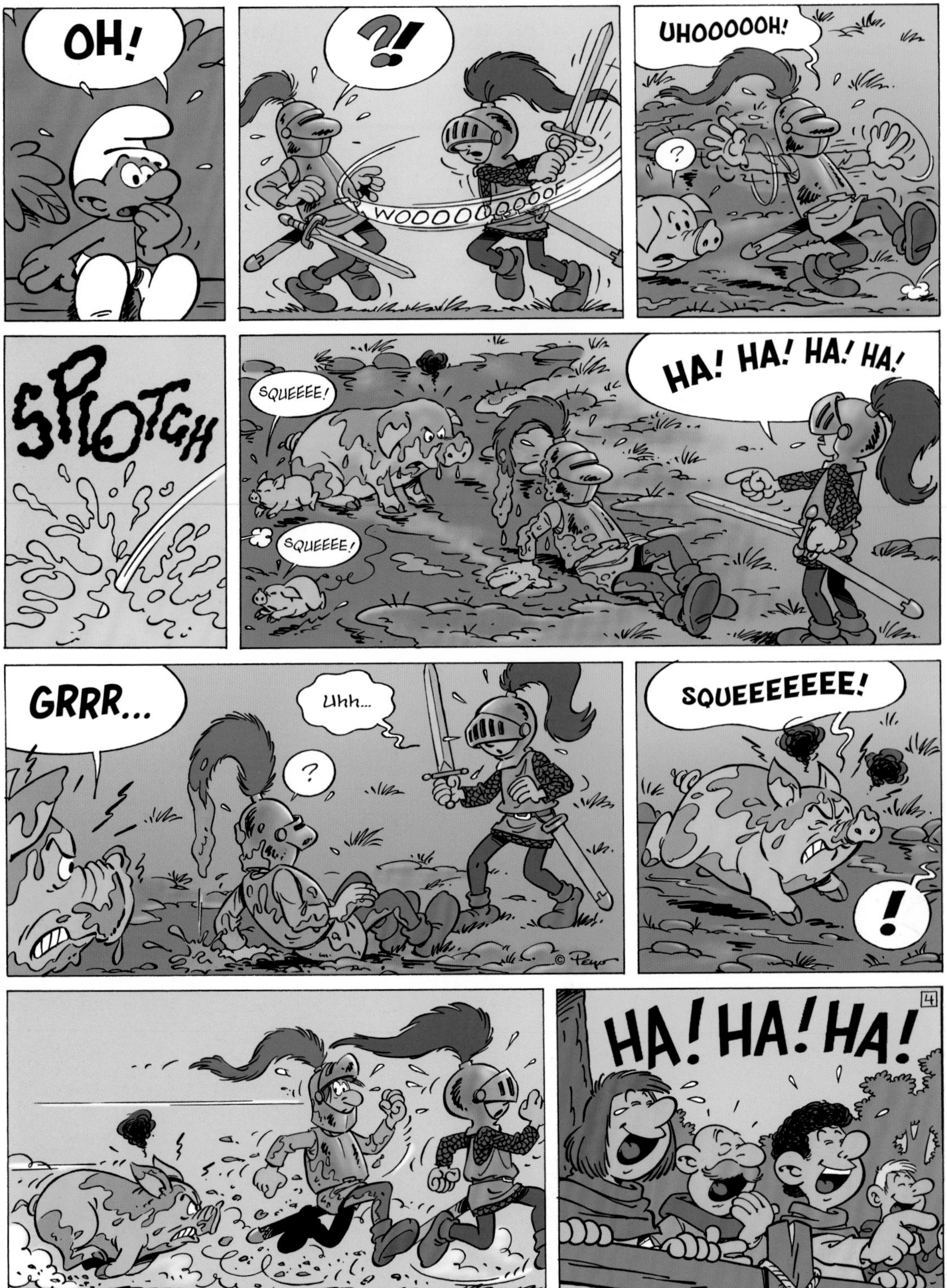
OH!
?!
WOOOOOOOOOF
UHOOOOOH!
?
SPLOTCH
SQUEEEE!
SQUEEEE!
HA! HA! HA! HA!
GRRR...
Uhh...
?
© Peyo
SQUEEEEEEE!
!
4
HA! HA! HA!

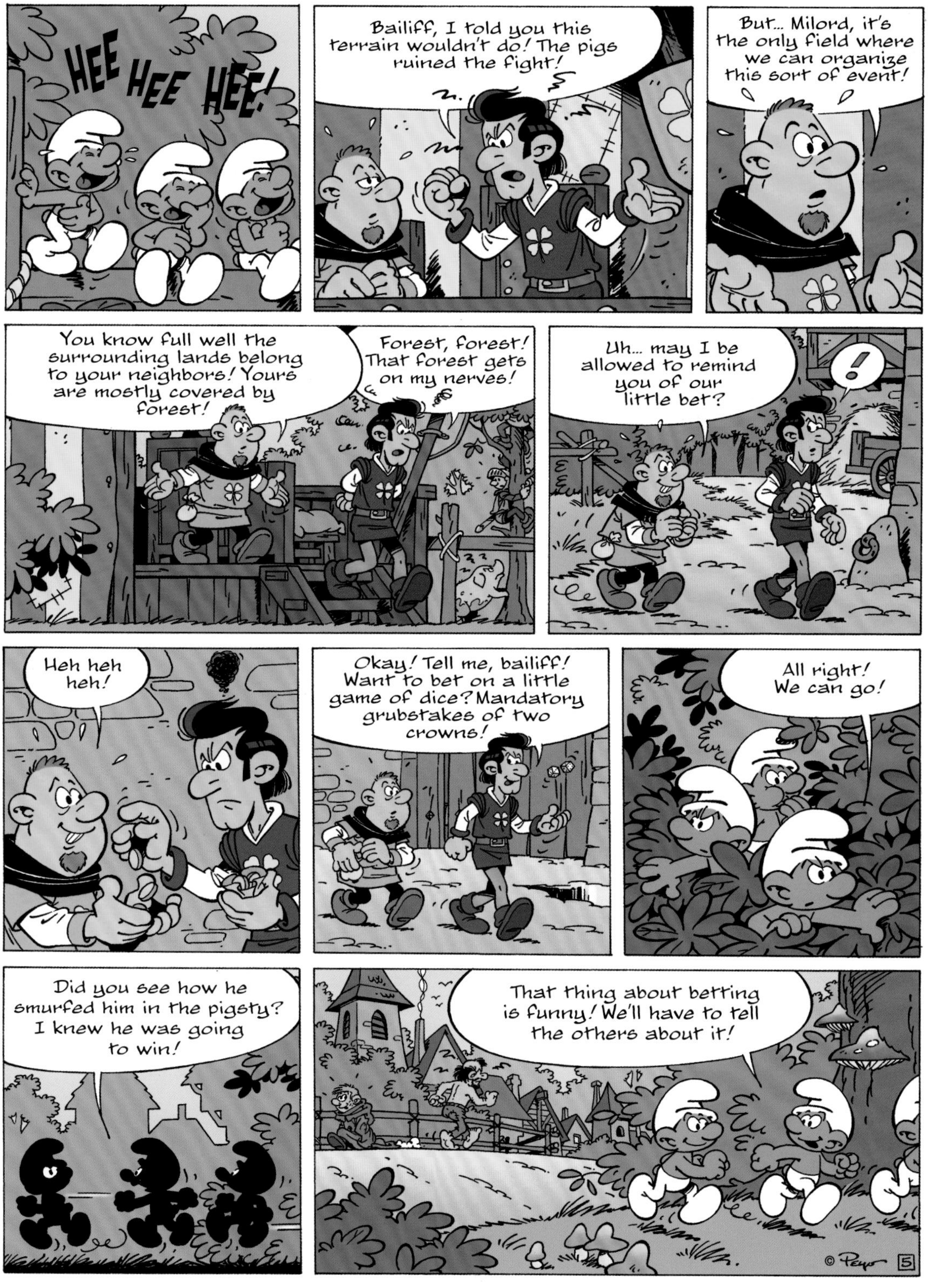

HEE HEE HEE!
Bailiff, I told you this terrain wouldn't do! The pigs ruined the fight!
But... Milord, it's the only field where we can organize this sort of event!
You know full well the surrounding lands belong to your neighbors! Yours are mostly covered by forest!
Forest, forest! That forest gets on my nerves!
Uh... may I be allowed to remind you of our little bet?
!
Heh heh heh!
Okay! Tell me, bailiff! Want to bet on a little game of dice? Mandatory grubstakes of two crowns!
All right! We can go!
Did you see how he smurfed him in the pigsty? I knew he was going to win!
That thing about betting is funny! We'll have to tell the others about it!
© Peyo
5

Later, at the Smurf Village... What are they doing? They've been gone a long time!

Ah! There they are!

WHAT?! You forgot the spices? How will I smurf my recipe now?

Well... we got them in town, then we smurfed them near the field, but we forgot them there!

Could we still have our extra desserts, Chef Smurf?

Your desserts?! Go look near the field and see if they're there!

Well, I guess we can cross that one off our smurf! I'd been dreaming about it for two days!

→PFF!←... Chef Smurf sure isn't very nice!

POC

!

BONG

Hey, did you see that smurfy shot?

Mmm, yeah... Pure luck!

PURE LUCK?! What do you bet I can resmurf it?

It's a bet!

I'm sure you won't!

We'll see about that!

© Peyo

6

TOC

OOPS!

HUP! HUP!

BOP

→Arrgh!← ...Darn, missed!

Hee hee hee! You lost your bet!

?

Uh... Well, I bet that, in a few moments, you'll smurf a black eye!

?

!

Who smurfed that rock?

I don't see what's so funny!

Okay, but I won my bet!

© Peyo

Wait for me here, I have an idea!

?

A few moments later...

DICE! AWESOME!

You'll see, I'm the king of dice! And this time, no more smurfing bets without any stakes!

CLIK CLIK CLAK

Agreed! I have three hazelnuts I smurfed in town this morning!

I must have one or two left too!

Uh... I already smurfed all of mine!

If you don't have anything to bet, you can't smurf dice with us!

That's not fair! I want to smurf, too!

I must have something left in my pocket!

AH! The cookie I lost last week!

Yuck! It's all soft! You already smurfed it!

Bah! It's just for a snack!

All right! It's okay to bet it this time!

Look out, I bet I smurf a seven! Here goes!

CLIK

SEVEN! I WIN!

© Peyo

8

150

Seven again? That's the third time!

?

Hey! What are you smurfing?

CLIK CLIK CLIK

We're smurfing dice! But Smurf is so lucky he already smurfed almost everything from us! He's a lucky dog!

Uh oh! That's easy to say!

CLIK CLIK CLIK

That looks like fun! How does it work? Can I smurf with you?

Of course, so long as you have something to wager!

Soon after...

Ha! Ha! Ha! Ha! You only smurfed a five that time! You lost and I'm pocketing all the bets!

Well, darn it!

What do you mean "lost"? I bet on you 'cause you told me you never lose!

I smurfed back my cookie!

?

I don't understand. Usually I smurf a seven every time!

But... what about the ladder then?

Sorry, what's been wagered and lost isn't smurfed back!

TAP TAP

!

© Peyo

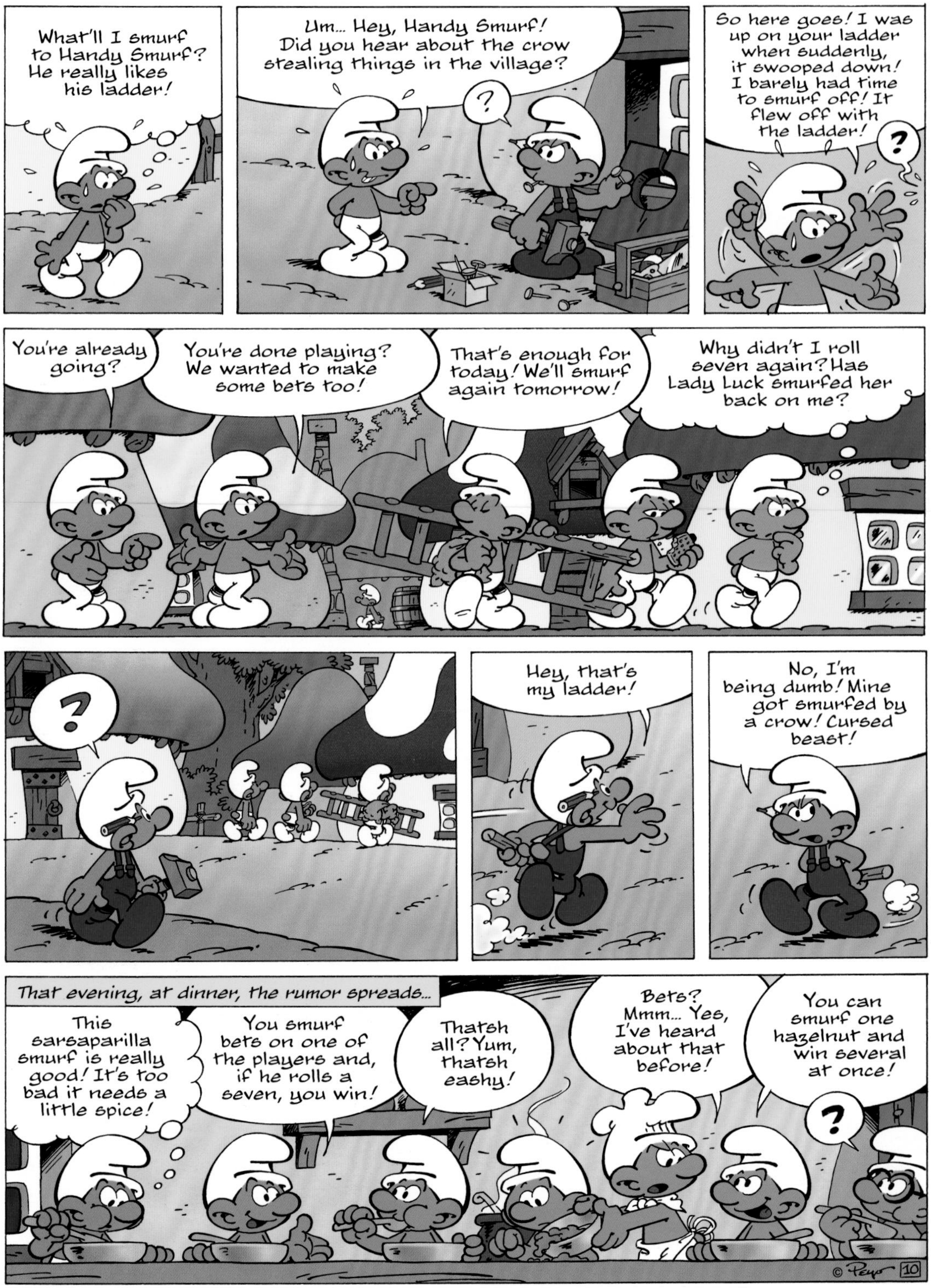
What'll I smurf to Handy Smurf? He really likes his ladder!
Um... Hey, Handy Smurf! Did you hear about the crow stealing things in the village?
?
So here goes! I was up on your ladder when suddenly, it swooped down! I barely had time to smurf off! It flew off with the ladder!
?
You're already going?
You're done playing? We wanted to make some bets too!
That's enough for today! We'll smurf again tomorrow!
Why didn't I roll seven again? Has Lady Luck smurfed her back on me?
?
Hey, that's my ladder!
No, I'm being dumb! Mine got smurfed by a crow! Cursed beast!
That evening, at dinner, the rumor spreads...
This sarsaparilla smurf is really good! It's too bad it needs a little spice!
You smurf bets on one of the players and, if he rolls a seven, you win!
Thatsh all? Yum, thatsh eashy!
Bets? Mmm... Yes, I've heard about that before!
You can smurf one hazelnut and win several at once!
?
© Peyo 10

And the next day...

Papa Smurf is really busy lately!

I'll help him out by taking a little tour of the village and seeing if everything's all right!

?

Go ahead, you can bet anything at all!

I don't know if I should bet my mirror! It's my most precious possession after all!

Today, I feel like I'm going to smurf lots of sevens!

CLIK CLIK CLIK

Of course, you may bet your trumpet! So long as you stop smurfing it!

POUAAK

© Peyo

Uh... if you could just win this time! I'd really like to smurf that ladder back, it's important!

Don't worry, it's in the bag!

I have a new trick for smurfing my luck back! I smurf once on the ground, and...

PTOOEY!

CLIK CLIK

FOUR! You lose!

AGAIN?! But I bet my furniture! Are you sure you really smurfed on the ground, Lucky Smurf?

Maybe I should've smurfed two times instead of once!

Sorry, you lost your furniture!

Yippee! I won! I bet that he'd miss!

Me, I don't like losing!

Well now? What's this? You should be at the bridge smurfing repairs!

Darn! Here's the party-pooper!

I lost my furniture!

WHAT?! You're smurfing dice? I'm going to tell Papa Smurf!

In fact, I'll do so right now!

You rotten tattle-tale!

TIC

TIC

TIC

SEVEN! Well, you win the roll, Brainy Smurf!

!

Oh, yeah? And uh... what were the stakes?

Later...

Laboratory

NO SMURFING

÷Yawn!÷ Enough work! A little nap will do me good!

HEY! WATCH OUT!

BUMP

OOPS! Sorry, Papa Smurf! I didn't see you!

Is that you, Brainy Smurf? What happened to you? Where are your clothes? And your glasses?

Uh... Let's just say...

Excuse me, but I have a meeting to smurf and I'm running late!

?

That was strange behavior even for Brainy Smurf!

PAT PAT

© Peyo

12

154

Hello, Papa Smurf! Don't you think these glasses smurf marvelous on me?

?!

TR!!!

There's something funny going on here!

Soon, the gambling frenzy grips the whole village...

For smurf's sake! Already? I'm late!

Okay, my hat, my pickaxe, my shovel...

Mustn't forget my lantern!

Quick! Quick!

Hello, Papa Smurf!

Uh... Hello!

Excuse me, I'm running late!

It does me good to see a Smurf taking his job seriously! Aaah... if only they could all be like him!

Wait! Don't start without me. I brought lots of stuff to wager!

What's going on? You're not smurfing dice anymore?

13

We found a new game to bet on! Snail races!

I bet everything on number three!

Hurry up! Smurf your bets! The race will start soon!

That's it! All betting is closed! **HERE GOES!**

SMURF THE LETTUCE!

YIPPEEEE! They're off!

Faster! Faster!

LET'S GO! GO, NUMBER FOUR!

?

What?! You, Smurfette?! You're smurfing bets too?

Uh... Not at all! I'm just here to make sure the snails aren't mistreated!

Much, much later...

Number four wins!

Uh, hey... The race is over!

Available soon at your local libraries and booksellers.

156

WATCH OUT FOR PAPERCUTZ

"Hello, I Must Be Going." –sung by Groucho Marx as Captain Spaulding in the 1930 film, Animal Crackers

Welcome to THE SMURFS TALES #7 by Peyo, featuring the little blue stars of the hit Nickelodeon TV series, as well as *Benny Breakiron* and *Johan and Peewit* (those other classic Peyo creations, on an alternating basis), all brought to you by Papercutz—those Smurftastic folks dedicated to publishing great graphic novels for all ages. I'm Jim Salicrup, the erstwhile Editor-in-Chief and Smurf Fan, here to share some really big Papercutz news...

Alas, it was already reported on Forbes.com that Papercutz has been purchased by Mad Cave Studios. This is great news, as it means Papercutz will not only continue to bring you the graphic novels you already love but will also launch even more. And Mad Cave Studios has the resources to do an even better job of promoting and marketing Papercutz and getting our graphic novels onto the shelves of even more booksellers and libraries, both print and digital editions.

The new Papercutz Editorial Director is Rex Ogle, who has worked at Marvel and DC Comics, as well as Scholastic and Little, Brown for Young Readers. He's worked on everything from *LEGO* and *Minecraft* to *Star Wars* and *Buffy the Vampire Slayer*. When he's not editing books, he's either reading or writing them. Joining Rex will be Senior Editor Zohra Ashpari, who was previously an editor at Tapas Media and has worked within the editorial departments of Scholastic and Tor Books. And completing the new editorial team will be Assistant Editor Stephanie Brooks, who started as an editorial intern at NBM before becoming my Assistant Managing Editor at Papercutz. Welcome, Rex, Zohra, and Stephanie! The future of Papercutz is certainly in good hands!

Over twenty years ago, graphic novel pioneer and NBM publisher, Terry Nantier, had the brilliant concept of starting yet another graphic novel publishing company. When he originally launched NBM, the idea of comics for adults was revolutionary in the United States. After successfully proving that concept could succeed, he noticed that almost every comics publisher was then aiming their comics to the adult audience, virtually abandoning kids. That's when Terry realized that there should be comics for kids again, especially for girls, and the idea for Papercutz was born. The name Papercutz was dreamed up by Terry's daughter Sylvia, who specifically requested that it not be spelled with a "Z" at the end, but you know how dads can be. That's also around the time that Terry asked me to be his partner and Editor-in-Chief in this crazy new venture, for which I readily agreed. I had started at Marvel Comics in 1972 when I was fifteen years old (2022 marked my 50th anniversary of working in comics!). The year before that, I was one of the kids at Kid's Magazine. Seems I've always been interested in comics for kids. Even at Marvel I had written and then edited SPIDEY SUPER STORIES, a kids' version of *Spider-Man* comics designed to help children read, co-produced with the producers of *Sesame Street* and *The Electric Company*: the Children's Television Workshop. And there were countless other kids-oriented projects that I worked on over the years.

The first Papercutz comic book, THE HARDY BOYS, was published in 2004, and in 2005, the first Papercutz graphic novels, THE HARDY BOYS and NANCY DREW saw print. And we've been at it ever since, through a world-wide Great Recession in 2008 and the recent global COVID Pandemic. But after almost twenty years Terry and I decided it was time for others to take Papercutz up to the next level, and that's where Mad Cave Studios comes in. While there was virtually no competition in the kids graphic novel category when we started, now almost every comics and book publisher is producing graphic novels for kids. Mad Cave Studios is better equipped to handle that kind of fierce competition.

For Terry and me, it's a little like Papercutz is one of our children that has grown up and is going off to college. While we both will still be around for a while as consultants to make the transition go as smoothly as possible, eventually we'll be moving on, leaving our child in the very capable hands of Mad Cave Studios. While I may be leaving Papercutz, I'm certainly not leaving comics. There've been may other projects I've been hoping to work on, but Papercutz had been taking up almost every waking hour of my time. Now I'll be free to work on those projects.

There are way too many people I'd like to thank for making my time at Papercutz over the years so wonderful. Terry, of course, the best publishing partner I could ever imagine! All of our writers, artists, letterers, colorists, production people, and of course, my invaluable, hard-working Managing Editors Michael Petranek, Bethany Bryan, Suzannah Rowntree, Jeff Whitman, and Stephanie Brooks. And of course, all of you, the Papercutz fans who have supported us over the years, with a special shout out to Rachel Boden, one our biggest fans.

This will also be my final *Watch Out* for the Papercutz column in THE SMURFS TALES, but in light of the great news regarding Mad Cave Studios taking over, may my last words simply be, watch out for Papercutz—the best is yet to come!
Thanks,

STAY IN TOUCH!
WEB: papercutz.com
TWITTER: @papercutzgn
FACEBOOK: PAPERCUTZGRAPHICNOVELS
Go to papercutz.com and sign up for the free Papercutz e-newsletter!

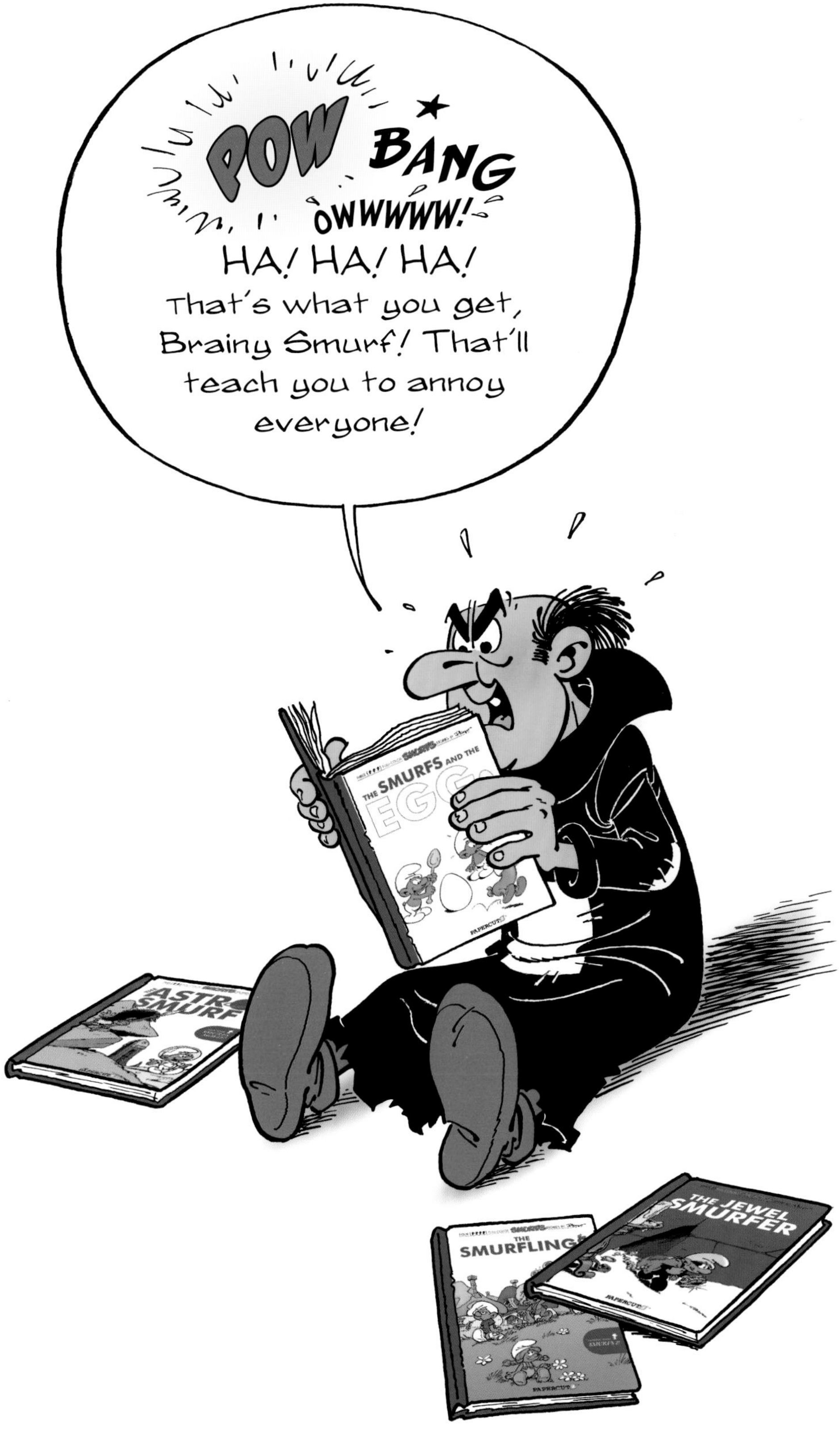
POW
BANG
OWWWWW!
HA! HA! HA!
That's what you get, Brainy Smurf! That'll teach you to annoy everyone!
THE SMURFS AND THE EGG
PAPERCUTZ
THE ASTROSMURF
THE SMURFLINGS
PAPERCUTZ
THE JEWEL SMURFER
PAPERCUTZ

THE SMURFS GRAPHIC NOVELS AVAILABLE FROM PAPERCUTZ

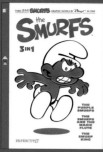

THE SMURFS 3 IN 1 VOL. 1

THE SMURFS 3 IN 1 VOL. 2

THE SMURFS 3 IN 1 VOL. 3

THE SMURFS 3 IN 1 VOL. 4

THE SMURFS 3 IN 1 VOL. 5

THE SMURFS 3 IN 1 VOL. 6

THE SMURFS 3 IN 1 VOL. 7

THE SMURFS 3 IN 1 VOL. 8

THE SMURFS 3 IN 1 VOL. 9

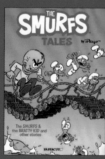

THE SMURFS TALES #1

THE SMURFS TALES #2

THE SMURFS TALES #3

THE SMURFS TALES #4

THE SMURFS TALES #5

THE SMURFS TALES #6

THE SMURFS TALES #7

THE SMURFS graphic novels are also available digitally from COMIXOLOGY.com as well as at ebook sellers everywhere.

WWW.PAPERCUTZ.COM

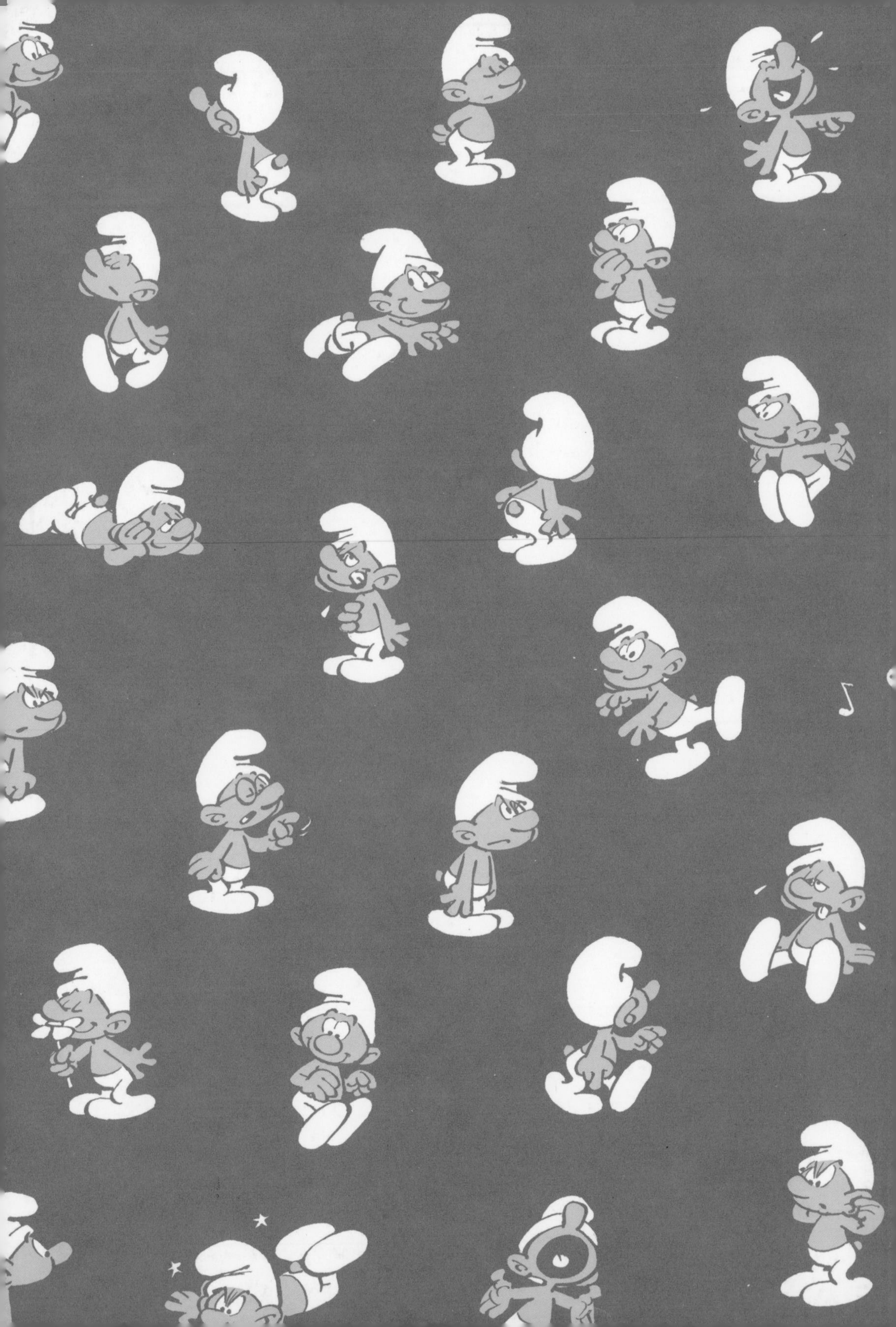